Praise for *Shade*

Blend atmospheric academic politics at Harvard University with a murder that rocks a New England community, and explores the gay lifestyle operating beneath its veneer of conservatism, for a sense of the different approach that *Shade* cultivates. . . .

Describing *Shade* as a "murder mystery" alone does it an injustice. Few books would tackle the conundrum presented by the outcome of a murder probe that reveals forces of corruption alongside the draw of a love destined to change everything. These elements set *Shade* apart from most other murder mysteries, giving it a boost that makes it **highly recommended**. —D. Donovan

Senior Reviewer, *Midwest Book Review*

In H. N. Hirsch's *Shade*, Marcus George, a junior faculty member at Harvard who is gay and in almost every way an outsider, gets drawn into solving the murder of one of his advisees, the son—gay, brilliant, and gorgeous—of an old, elite Massachusetts family. This is a mystery that . . . capture[s] the tense, competitive world of academic politics.

The plot thickens and thickens again, and in the process, Marcus falls into a tender and heartwarming love affair. **A gripping read** from beginning to end. —Priscilla Long

author, *The Writer's Portable Mentor*

Shade is **a dilly of a mystery!** Set in mid-1980s ivory-tower academia, a gay, untenured Harvard professor discovers that "publish or perish" can lead to dark places when he is asked to help find the murderer of a gifted former student. Hirsch brilliantly captures the milieux of Boston and the very rich, the dog-eat-dog world of faculty hierarchy, and gay life at the beginning of AIDS' deadly march.

The dénouement is part of the fun of this entertaining and insightful novel, a congenial fillip for those who enjoy mysteries.

—C. Robert Jones
author, *The Mystery at Claggett Cove*

Pisgah Press was established in 2011 to publish and promote works of quality offering original ideas and insight into the human condition and the world around us.

Published by Pisgah Press, LLC
PO Box 9663, Asheville, NC 28815
www.pisgahpress.com

Book design: A. D. Reed, MyOwnEditor.com

Library of Congress Cataloging-in-Publication Data
Hirsch, Harry N.

.
Shade/H.N. Hirsch
Library of Congress Control Number: 2022937051

ISBN: 978-1-942016-68-7

First Edition
June 2022
Printed in the United States of America

Shade

H. N. Hirsch

Pisgah Press
Asheville, NC IP

Shade

At first he did not think it would be anything, just a quick meal with a former student. He didn't know a young life was about to end, or that his own life was, in a way, just beginning.

1

Marcus George stood on the stairs of Widener Library, halfway up, waiting. He was sweating, more from nerves than from the early-summer heat, though he cursed himself for wearing his corduroy jacket, the sort of jacket that was almost a requirement at Harvard in the eighties, part of the uniform of a serious young scholar.

He tried to think of something cool and refreshing and looked around at the old, graceful trees. Harvard Yard was full of people lounging on the grass, talking, laughing. Summer school students were eating bag lunches on the steps of Memorial Church. As usual, he envied the nonchalance of the young.

Two colleagues smiled at him from the bottom of the stairs. Marcus smiled back, his best junior faculty smile, and gave a little wave. They were no doubt on their way to the faculty club for lunch: Deena Echols, newly tenured, and Sidney Hawley, who had been at Harvard for decades. Deena's smile was tight, dismissive; she had been friendly toward Marcus while she was a lowly untenured assistant professor, but now she was one of the elect and had no time for him. Harvard was full of these subtle signs of its class system. To look busy, Marcus pretended to shuffle some papers in the outside pocket of his briefcase.

Damn preppy. Where the hell is he?

He put his briefcase down on the concrete, loosened his tie, then picked up the briefcase, walked to the bottom of the steps, and considered the rest of his day. PhD oral at 3:00. The obligatory drink after. Then home, alone, as usual.

Looking around Harvard Yard, Marcus wondered how much longer he would have a place here. He glanced up at the library entrance, thought about going to his carrel, but it was just a wire cage looking out on a dreary courtyard, not a real office like those given to the senior faculty. *No*, he thought, *I can't sit in there right now, too depressing, I'll grab lunch by myself.*

And then he saw Trip emerge from the library entrance at the top of the stairs. He was tan, wearing a polo shirt and chinos, and looked like a model for Banana Republic. He was smiling broadly and waved.

His full name was Addison Cornell Howard III, but everyone called him Trip. Marcus remembered smiling to himself when he first saw the name on his class roster—a true blue blood. Three names, all interchangeable, were the sure sign. It could be three first names, like David Herbert Donald, one of the more eminent Harvard historians, or three last names, like Endicott Peabody Saltonstall, an alum and politician after whom a senior prize had been named. Either way, three interchangeable names were a dead giveaway. Marcus might have been in the club himself except that his parents hadn't bothered to give him a middle name, he'd grown up working-class, and he was Jewish.

He'd assumed Trip would be the usual spoiled preppy, slightly sneering, above it all, a varsity athlete who cared nothing for his classes, knowing his future was secure. But Trip was different. He was a serious student, diligent, always prepared, insightful, and he wrote concise, razor-sharp essays. Marcus had been the adviser for his senior honors thesis on Abraham Lincoln, and Trip had just graduated *magna cum laude*. He had written a bold and interesting thesis, tying Lincoln's early, possibly homoerotic relationship with Joshua Speed to his later ideas about brotherhood and fraternity. It was a subtle work, delicately written, not overplaying the possibility of a physical relationship between Lincoln and Speed, but not underplaying it either. It was well done, original.

Trip was openly, proudly gay, and stunningly beautiful to boot. Tall, muscular, with light brown hair that turned blond in the summer and a smile that could win him the elective office he would no doubt someday seek, continuing the family tradition. His older brother was already a state senator. Among his ancestors were well-known figures from Massachusetts history on both sides of the family, including a U.S. senator, a governor, and a famous abolitionist.

Marcus hadn't been able to suppress the jolt of attraction he felt looking at Trip, listening to him speak in class or one on one during office hours. He tried not to let it show, of course, but they seemed to be playing the usual game. *Yes, I know you're attracted to me*, Trip's manner subtly suggested, *but we won't discuss that or do anything about it. Yes, I know you're gorgeous and gay*, Marcus telegraphed, *but you're a student and I'm a professor, end of story*. It was a game Marcus had played before, sometimes reluctantly, sometimes willingly, and by now he recognized its contours and rules.

So he was surprised when Trip wrote him just after graduation and suggested they meet for lunch. There was something he needed advice about, he said, and Marcus assumed it would be a request for a letter of recommendation or the usual law school talk: Should I go now or wait and work for a few years before applying, how do I prepare for the LSAT, should I aim for Harvard or Yale, or should I be daring and try Berkeley or Michigan? Funny how well-off, well-connected Harvard students thought applying to the Berkeley or Michigan law schools was a bold, risky step.

Trip greeted Marcus warmly, and they made small talk as they walked to Harvard Square, the weather, the recent graduation speech by the chair of the Federal Reserve, the latest political news. Trip seemed nervous, talking faster than usual and speaking deferentially, without his customary self-assurance. He suggested a small, quiet restaurant just off Harvard Square, and they settled in.

"So, what have you been doing?" Marcus asked after they ordered.

"I'm spending the summer up in Miller's Cove," Trip said. "I'm just in Boston for a day or two."

Miller's Cove was a modest resort on the coast of Maine, about two hours north of Boston. It had a small gay colony and a few gay venues, but was supposed to be much more subdued than raucous Provincetown. Trip's family had a place on the coast a bit farther south, he said, in Kennebunkport, near Vice President Bush's family compound, and staying in Miller's Cove allowed him to put in the requisite appearance or two without spending the entire summer surrounded by his parents and Republicans. He described his family home in some detail and told a funny story about meeting George Bush once, before he was vice-president, and spilling the lemonade Barbara offered him.

"I'm going to be up in Miller's Cove in a few weeks

myself," Marcus said.

"Oh, that's great. Have you been there before?" Trip seemed genuinely pleased.

Marcus said he hadn't, that he had always wanted to try it out. "I made a reservation at one of the B and Bs. The Hilltop Inn."

"Yes, I know that place. I can show you around."

Their food arrived. Marcus had skipped breakfast and dove into his salad, but Trip barely touched his omelet. Marcus waited for whatever it was Trip wanted to discuss, but the law school questions never came, nor did anything else of import. They chatted about this and that, nothing but small talk.

As they left the restaurant, Trip said, "When you come up to Miller's Cove, there's something I need to talk to you about."

Marcus felt a twinge of impatience—why hadn't Trip just brought it up, whatever it was, over lunch? But he knew that undergraduates had their own internal compasses, that they sometimes needed to test out whether a faculty member could be trusted with personal information before actually revealing it.

They parted in Harvard Square, in front of the Coop. "Be sure to call me when you get in," Trip said, and gave Marcus the number.

Much later, Marcus would pore over every detail of that afternoon. Had he missed something, some clue that might have saved Trip's life?

2

Marcus passed the next few weeks in the usual early-summer daze, sleeping late, depressurizing from the academic year, reading, making notes for the book he was supposed to be writing but not actually writing it. He had already published his dissertation, on the rhetoric of American law in the early twentieth century, and it had received respectable reviews, but he knew he needed a second book fast if he was to have a prayer of tenure at Harvard. He had announced that he would write a book on mid-nineteenth-century American political thought, looking at both fiction and nonfiction, Emerson, Thoreau, Hawthorne, Melville, but so much had already been written about the period that once he got going, he despaired. How in the world was he supposed to say anything original?

That was the curse of his field, American political and legal thought: it was well-trodden ground. He loved the material, enjoyed teaching it, but producing a steady stream of original scholarship? Really? His program, History and Literature, was full of luminaries who churned out books and articles the way Hollywood churned out movies. Marcus would dutifully read primary sources and come up with an idea that seemed original, and then he'd read the secondary literature and find that someone had already made the same argument that had seemed so fresh and exciting to him.

A sardonic friend who taught film once quoted Woody Allen's line that the three worst words in the English language were "Let's be friends." For an academic, his friend said, the three worst words were "It's been done."

Harvard, which made its own rules, didn't have a tenure-track system; junior faculty were hired on five-year contracts as assistant professors. If you did well, they added three more years as an untenured associate professor. Marcus would be entering his fourth year in the fall—the year his colleagues would decide if he deserved the three-year add-on. After that, to be tenured, you had to be considered one of the very best in the entire world in your particular subfield, and that was a tall order, difficult to achieve in only eight years no matter how smart you were, what with teaching and advising and committee work. Perhaps one in twelve made it through; Deena Echols was the latest to be anointed from within. When Marcus was a graduate student at Princeton and his adviser put him up for the Harvard job, he had only the vaguest idea of what he might be getting into.

Being denied tenure at Harvard didn't mean the end of your career, Marcus knew; everyone, or most everyone, went on to very decent academic posts elsewhere, usually with tenure, or with tenure in a year or two. But eight years was just enough time to feel settled, and he had watched slightly older colleagues go through the trauma of having to leave a job, friends, a life.

Not that Marcus had much of a life. He had friends, to be sure, but he had not yet found Him, the One. He'd had an affair or two, nice men, and Marcus would have liked to go further, but something just didn't click. He had gone into therapy to try to figure out why, but so far that had only added to his muddle. The therapist was fond of Zen aphorisms, and would say things like "You can never step into the same river twice." Half the time Marcus had no idea what he was talking about or how it applied to his situation, and he'd leave the session more confused than when he walked in. He was beginning to resent the therapy; it was expensive, and Harvard did not pay well. You were supposed to live on prestige, Marcus assumed, or on your private income or your spouse's, neither of which Marcus had. But he also knew that resenting the therapist might be part of what was supposed to happen, so he stuck to it.

During the weeks before leaving for Maine, Marcus would sometimes have dinner at one of the cheap restaurants in Cambridge and then find his way to the Paradise, a low-key bar, working-class by day, gay after dark. He'd order a glass of club soda or sometimes wine and stand awkwardly against a back wall, waiting for something to happen, or for the courage to strike up a conversation. The courage seldom arrived.

There were places where Marcus felt safe, in his element—the classroom especially, and on the streets of Cambridge or at the library—and places where he felt like a sparrow in a tornado—Harvard receptions, faculty meetings, and gay bars. At the bars he knew he needed to look cool and confident, but instead he felt awkward and silly. And his body's natural rhythm didn't help; he often went to these places too early and was ready for sleep by 10:30, when they just started to fill up.

On those rare occasions when he was feeling particularly brave, he would drive across the river to one of Boston's gay bars. They were glitzier, the music was louder, the crowd better dressed, but he seldom stayed more than half an hour. He would drive home feeling like his friend in the anthropology department who traveled for five days from Rio to study an obscure native tribe in Brazil, only to be told by the chief, who spoke English, to get lost.

In gay bars Marcus began to understand what some of his students meant when they talked about throwing shade. In a bar Marcus would smile at someone or give them an appreciative, hopeful look, only to be met with rolled eyes or a stiffened neck or a mocking toss of the head. He'd know instantly he was being told the same thing as his anthropologist friend: Get lost.

He loved the phrase "throwing shade," which he had just discovered in a student's paper, one that was prodigiously researched. The first use of the term "shade," the student discovered, turned out to be in Jane Austen's *Mansfield Park* in 1814, when a character takes a dinner guest to task for a disparaging remark that seems to be "throwing shade on the Admiral." By the 1980s, the phrase was becoming popular in gay and drag communities in the U.S., especially in the highly organized drag subculture of New York. This was one of the reasons Marcus loved his field, the exploration of the connections between literary works and popular culture. The student who wrote that paper had a great future in front of him, and he was one of the few students Marcus encouraged to think about a PhD.

On June 27, Marcus packed and drove up to Miller's Cove for his three-week vacation. He was relieved to get out of Cambridge and his hot little apartment on Kirkland Street.

He could see that it was a lovely little town as soon as he arrived. He settled into his B and B, which sat on a hill overlooking the town's central intersection, and was delighted to find that his small room had a view of the water a few blocks away. The bathroom was shared, and hot water was sometimes in short supply, the owner told him as he showed him around, but Marcus didn't mind. There were several decks and a pool, and in the morning Marcus took his coffee and his blueberry muffin or bagel out onto one of the decks, where he read the local newspapers and the *New York Times* and chatted with the other guests. The clientele was a mix of gay men and French Canadians, and it was charming to come down to breakfast and hear French being spoken.

The beach was stunning. A ten-minute walk from the inn, it stretched out along the shoreline with its clean, almost white sand. Its width varied enormously with the high and low tide, and there was something hypnotic about watching the water slowly recede or come in. The water was cold, ice cold, almost too cold for swimming.

At the entrance to the beach stood a modern hotel. Next to it, right up against the sand, was a long row of benches under a graceful cloth awning. Marcus headed there in late morning, stopping at a deli to buy a sandwich for lunch and a large bottle of water. At the local drugstore he bought sunscreen and insect repellant and doused himself; he burned easily, and mosquitoes seemed to zero in on him with kamikaze accuracy.

During those first few innocent days, Marcus enjoyed sitting under the awning with whatever book he was reading and a pad and pen. The awning provided just enough cover to help protect him from sunburn, and he was able to make some useful notes for his book. When he needed a break or wanted to think about what he had just read, he set his things on the bench and asked someone sitting nearby to watch them; it was often a French Canadian mother or father with a young child. Then he walked out along the shoreline to what everyone called Section B, for boys, where the gay men congregated.

All the boys there, and the few girls, seemed to be in groups of two or three, but Marcus didn't mind being alone; he had realized in graduate school that being a scholar meant long solitary stretches of time reading, thinking, writing. He'd smile at people he recognized from the inn, and some gave a friendly wave.

Marcus loved the ocean as perhaps only someone who grew up without it can. In Chicago there was the lake, of course, and it was beautiful, but the ocean was different: the smell, the gulls, the tide coming in and going out, the sound of the waves. After a few days he began to relax, even with the noisy Fourth of July crowds swirling around him.

Maybe he'd found a place he could love, he thought to himself. He didn't even mind having dinner alone in one of the local restaurants. He especially liked Maineium's, an old-fashioned diner with red leather booths and a soda fountain.

On the afternoon of the Fourth, the gay couple who ran the inn held a cocktail party and picnic for friends, guests, and some locals. Marcus usually hated occasions like that, hated trying to make small talk with people he didn't know, but this time he enjoyed himself. Maybe it was the effect of the ocean, or maybe he was loosening up. The weather helped; it was a perfect summer day, warm but not muggy, a cool breeze coming off the shore. When it got dark and the fireworks started they heard sirens and wondered what was happening, but the sound faded quickly.

Marcus went off to bed feeling content. As he fell asleep, his volume of Emerson essays fell to the floor. "Good night, Waldo," he said out loud, and smiled as he drifted off.

The next morning Marcus slept unusually late, and when

he finally roused himself it was chilly and raining. He put on a cotton sweater and made his way down to the pastries and coffee, thinking it might be a good time to call Trip. During the first few days he couldn't decide whether he should call at all; he didn't want to seem too forward with a former student. But it was a small town, they were bound to run into each other, and Trip might be offended if Marcus hadn't been in touch, so why not call him, meet for coffee? Besides, Trip apparently had something he wanted to talk over, something that troubled him, though he'd been reluctant to spill the beans in Cambridge.

It was still raining, and someone said it was supposed to keep up all day. Marcus used the inn's courtesy phone to dial the number Trip had handed him in Cambridge.

An unfamiliar male voice answered. Marcus assumed it was Trip's roommate, or housemate, or perhaps boyfriend.

"May I speak to Trip? This is Marcus George, from Cambridge."

Marcus thought he heard a slight gasp at the other end of the line, and then the voice said, "Just a minute." After some sort of conversation in the background, a different unfamiliar voice came onto the line.

"This is Lieutenant Fitzgerald, Miller's Cove police. Who is this?"

"Police? What's happened?" Marcus felt panic in his stomach, but he tried to keep his voice steady.

The lieutenant repeated himself. "Who is this, and what is your relationship to Addison Howard?"

Marcus explained. As usual, the mention of Harvard produced default respect. The lieutenant's voice softened.

"I'm sorry to tell you, Professor George, that Addison Howard was found dead last night."

3

Marcus spent the rest of the morning in a daze and later couldn't remember what he did or didn't do. It was raining hard, so he couldn't have gone to the beach. He had a vague memory of going into the living room at the inn after hearing the news and just sitting there in an overstuffed chair, stunned. Perhaps he sat there for hours as the other guests drifted in and out. The only thing he could remember clearly was a young French Canadian couple, a man and a woman, playing cards at one of the small tables. They were young, happy, clearly in love. Marcus resented their happiness; it felt out of place. Didn't they know that the day, the month, maybe the year, was ruined?

At lunchtime he walked over to Maineium's. He ordered a grilled cheese, but his stomach was in knots and he ate very little. At two, as Lieutenant Fitzgerald had requested, he headed to the police station for an interview. He put on khaki pants, the first time he'd worn long pants since arriving in Miller's Cove. They felt strange and they got wet in the rain.

Marcus learned quickly that Trip's death was a homicide. He'd been found dead under the awning at the entrance to the beach.

He had been shot point-blank in the head. When Marcus

heard that, he closed his eyes for a moment and felt bile rising into his throat.

Lieutenant Fitzgerald asked him the usual questions: How long had he known Trip, in what capacity, when was the last time they spoke? Then came the questions Marcus dreaded but knew were coming: Do you know of any reason why someone might have wanted to harm him? Did he have any enemies? As far as you know, was anything bothering him?

Marcus described the lunch in Cambridge a few weeks before, and the lieutenant's interest was clearly aroused.

"Did you have any idea what Mr. Howard wanted to discuss? What was his manner? Did he seem distressed?"

Marcus could provide no useful information, and the lieutenant was clearly disappointed, but polite. As in hundreds of movies and TV shows, he thanked Marcus for coming in, handed him his card. "If you think of anything else about that lunch, Professor George, or anything else that might help us, any detail, please do not hesitate to call."

As the lieutenant walked Marcus to the door of the small squad room, Marcus asked if Trip's parents had been notified. They had; they'd be arriving shortly from Kennebunkport for an interview.

Outside the police station it was still raining, but not as hard. Marcus walked back to the center of town, trying to put his thoughts in order. He paused in front of the local bookstore, looked in the window, tried to calm his racing brain. The rain stopped and started; Marcus got soaked but didn't care.

It made absolutely no sense. A bright Harvard graduate from a prominent family, a sterling future in front of him, who could possibly have wanted him dead? There couldn't have been money problems. A robbery? A jealous boyfriend?

Marcus supposed either might be possible. A drug deal gone bad, like the unproven allegation in the local papers about the horrific murder of a gay teen in Boston the year before? Marcus didn't think that was likely; there was no hint at all that Trip had a drug problem, but you never knew.

Gay bashing by a local? Did gay bashers use a gun? Usually they just beat you up, and Miller's Cove seemed like an open and tolerant place, relying heavily on a large gay clientele for income, so that didn't seem likely either. And besides, on the Fourth of July by the beach, there must have been lots of people around.

Something else. But what?

Marcus wandered aimlessly. By late afternoon, back at the inn, he collapsed on his bed and fell immediately to sleep, as he usually did when bad news hit.

When he woke he felt drugged. It was nearly seven o'clock and he was hungry. He walked over to Maineium's, which was crowded, so he sat at the soda fountain and ordered some kind of unmemorable chicken. By that hour news of the murder had clearly spread; Marcus caught snatches of conversation about it as he paid his check. The young man behind the till, a sandy-haired local, asked if he had heard the news. Marcus nodded yes but said nothing more. He heard a waiter at a table behind him say that some people were so scared they were leaving town.

At the inn he went straight to bed, and by the next morning he knew what he was going to do. He wolfed down a bagel and coffee, got in his car, and headed for Kennebunkport, despite his better judgment. The sun was out, everything smelled fresh and sweet. Marcus hardly noticed.

4

It was a short drive, about fifteen minutes down the coast. He remembered Trip's description of the family's summer home, whitewashed clapboard, roses in front and a lap pool at the side, a few doors down from the beach, not far from the huge Bush compound.

It was easy enough to find. He didn't know if he was doing the right or appropriate thing, but he parked across the street, steeled his nerves, and rang the doorbell.

A slightly older version of Trip answered the door. The state senator, no doubt. Marcus introduced himself.

"Oh yes, Professor George, Trip mentioned you often. He said you were going to be in Miller's Cove. I'm David, his brother. Please come in."

He ushered Marcus into a large living room, airy, bright, decorated simply in white and blue. A lurking butler offered him coffee, which he gladly accepted.

He should have known there'd be a butler.

David excused himself. "I'll just go and get Father."

Marcus took the opportunity to survey the room. He noticed old books, a few tasteful glass bowls, and what looked a great deal like an original Turner above the fireplace, a painting of the tumultuous sea. He got up to look at the signature.

Sure enough. "JMWT." The thought crossed his mind: this one painting was probably worth more than Marcus would earn in a lifetime.

Addison Cornell Howard II came in and shook Marcus's hand. "It was kind of you to come," he said. He was tall, simply dressed, visibly grief-stricken. In a movie he would have been portrayed by Gregory Peck, equal parts Yankee respectability and country gentleman.

Marcus offered condolences. "It was a pleasure having Trip as a student," he said.

"Trip mentioned you often. He was excited about what he was doing, really enjoyed working with you. He was grateful for your help."

As they were talking, Trip's mother walked in. She was a strikingly beautiful woman, dressed in dark gray slacks and sweater, a single gold chain around her neck. She had been crying. Marcus rose, saying, "I'm so sorry." She smiled thinly and sat down on the white sofa next to her husband, who didn't look at her.

Marcus didn't know how to broach the topic of his lunch with Trip, but David reappeared and provided an opening.

"I wonder if you had any inkling of trouble in Trip's life, trouble of any kind?"

"Actually, there was something," Marcus said, and everyone was suddenly very still. David leaned slightly forward in his seat.

Marcus told them about the lunch in Cambridge, narrating it as accurately as he could from beginning to end.

"And you'll tell this to the police, no doubt?" David asked.

"Yes, of course, I already did. They interviewed me yesterday afternoon. I know it's not much to go on."

Trip's mother spoke for the first time. "Was he seeing anyone in Cambridge, could it have been related to that?" Her voice made Marcus think of Mia Farrow as Daisy Buchanan in the recent Hollywood version of *The Great Gatsby*, and of the line from the original novel, "Her voice was full of money." She even looked like Mia Farrow, if older, the same lovely eyes, the same subtly blond hair, no doubt dyed at this point in her life.

"He never said."

"Of course we knew that Trip was gay," Gregory Peck said. "He told us long ago, when he was at Andover. We had suspected, of course, and it took a little getting used to, but we had no problem with it. None at all." He sounded a bit like he was trying to convince himself as much as Marcus.

"We were glad he seemed so comfortable with who he was," Mia Farrow added with a faraway look in her eyes.

Marcus asked about the arrangements, and David said there would be a simple memorial service in a few weeks on the Harvard campus. Gregory Peck, Marcus knew, was on the Harvard Board of Overseers.

There was a strained silence, and then they fell to chatting about Miller's Cove, about the weather. The butler came in and announced a call from Mrs. Bush, who had offered condolences. No need to call her back, she'd said.

News travels fast, Marcus thought.

It was time to excuse himself. Mia Farrow took his hand in both of hers and thanked him for coming. She looked like she was about to start crying again. Trip's father and brother walked him to the front door, which the butler held open.

"I wonder if you might be willing to do something for us," David said. "The Miller's Cove police force is small, and we don't know how reliable they are. They can't be very well equipped for a murder investigation."

Marcus had had the same thought himself. He could sense that Mia Farrow was listening from the living room.

"We drove up to the Miller's Cove police station yesterday, and we were not at all impressed by Lieutenant Fitzgerald," the elder Howard put in. "Highly pedestrian questions, nothing that gave us confidence they could find the person who did this."

"You knew Trip well, and his world," David went on. "Could you possibly make inquiries in Miller's Cove and Cambridge, perhaps talk to Trip's friends, see if you might discover anything helpful?"

Trip's father was staring at Marcus intently. It was one of those moments in life when your body senses that something major is happening before it registers in your brain.

"Of course I'd like to do what I can," Marcus heard himself saying. "May I get back to you?"

"Certainly. Let us know," David said as he handed Marcus a card with four phone numbers.

5

On the drive back to Miller's Cove, Marcus considered. Part of him thought it was reasonable for Trip's family to ask him to look into things. After all, he had access to Trip's world in a way the family and the police did not. Trip had almost certainly told them Marcus was gay, given his thesis topic and how open Trip was.

The family probably thought there was a connection between Trip's sexuality and his murder. It was a somewhat homophobic but natural assumption, especially for people like that. What else could you expect from people who hung out with the Bushes? And they undoubtedly wanted a quiet investigation, in case it turned up something sordid, and trusted someone at Harvard to be discreet.

The other part of Marcus was annoyed. How typical that these Yankee bluebloods expected everyone else to do their bidding, like the tenured faculty at Harvard unloading the large undergraduate courses they didn't want to teach on the junior faculty. *I'm the hired help*, Marcus thought, *always will be*.

Except the family hadn't offered him money. He couldn't decide if he would have been flattered or insulted if they had.

And then Marcus remembered the anguished look on Mia Farrow's face and the sorrow hanging in the room like the scent of wilted flowers. They were a family in pain, and they had asked for his help. Even rich people sometimes needed help, and maybe they were right, maybe his connection to Trip and his world could uncover something.

Back in Miller's Cove, Marcus took a cup of coffee from the inn's tiny guest kitchen and sat out on the deck that surrounded the pool. He gagged a bit on the coffee, which had no doubt been sitting all morning and wasn't nearly as good as what he had been offered in Kennebunkport.

Guests were swimming, lounging, laughing, things that now felt as far away to Marcus as the moon.

He needed to think, and he always needed silence to think. Once, as an undergraduate at the University of Michigan working on his senior honors project, he had been toiling away for hours in a study carrel in the new wing of the graduate library, where the silence was profound—until someone in a nearby carrel started banging away on a typewriter. Marcus had nearly slugged the guy.

He left the noise of the inn and started walking, wrestling with the family's request. Why should he get himself mixed up with a murder investigation? Had Trip meant more to him than he realized? Did he think Trip was the victim of a hate crime and that he had a responsibility here as a gay man? Why did he feel a pull to get involved?

He didn't know, couldn't sort out his motives. And he shouldn't have to—he was on vacation, for the love of God. What did he know about crime? He should go back to Cambridge and write his goddamn book.

What goddamn book? It didn't exist, and maybe never would.

Back and forth he went, his head spinning. He walked around town, then to the beach, pacing up and down the shoreline while the tide was coming in, letting the cold water lap at his feet. He pictured Trip walking, swimming, laughing in the same spot.

In late afternoon, back at the inn, he took a long nap. When he woke, he was starving and realized he had skipped lunch. He went to Maineium's for an early dinner.

It was a lovely night, fragrant from the recent rain. A gentle breeze blew as Marcus returned to the inn and sat outside for a while, staring up at the stars.

How the hell did he get here? What was a gay boy from working-class Chicago doing teaching at Harvard, summering in Maine? Using "summer" as a verb was another sure sign of the upper crust, and Marcus laughed at himself. What would his grandparents, who'd escaped pogroms in Ukraine, think of him now? "We're a long way from Kiev, aren't we?" Marcus murmured out loud.

He went inside and called the first number on the card David Howard had given him, the one with a Maine area code.

David picked up on the first ring.

"I'll see what I can do," Marcus said.

"Thank you. Thank you so much. The family appreciates this. And of course let us know if there are any expenses."

As Marcus fell asleep he had two images in his head: his grandmother speaking Yiddish when he was a young boy, and the Turner over the Kennebunkport fireplace.

6

There was an obvious place to start looking into Trip's death: the house he'd apparently been sharing here, with the roommate who'd answered the phone when Marcus first called. By now the police would have been all over the place and questioned the roommate, Marcus knew. He doubted he'd find anything they hadn't, but the roommate was almost certainly gay, and Marcus had a personal connection to Trip, so perhaps the young man would open up and reveal something, anything, he hadn't told the police. The slightest detail in a case like this could be crucial. It was worth a shot.

Marcus called from the courtesy phone, and the same voice answered.

"Hello, this is Marcus George again. I was Trip's academic adviser at Harvard, and I've just seen his parents. I wonder if I could come by for a talk. Whenever it's convenient."

The voice answered unsteadily, clearly upset. "The police spent hours here yesterday tearing the place apart. I just finished cleaning up."

"Please, I only need a few minutes. Trip's parents have asked me to look into things, they're not sure they trust the local police."

There was a long pause.

"All right. Come by in an hour." The voice told Marcus where to find the house.

Marcus spent the hour by the pool reading the local paper, with its front-page story about the murder, full of lurid detail, the blood at the scene, the wealth of the family.

The house was on School Street, a small shingled cottage with a big front porch holding two comfortable-looking old wicker chairs. It was up a hill, and Marcus puffed as he made his way there. *I have to get in shape*, he told himself, as he'd been telling himself for a while, but he'd resisted the growing throng of gay men pumping away at gyms, although he did sometimes use one of the Harvard pools for a swim. Maybe that was why he wasn't more successful with men, he sometimes thought. His body wasn't a bad body, but it was too ordinary, not the sculpted, hairless block of granite that was becoming the gay norm.

He knocked on the cottage door. A slim young man with a head of unruly black curls opened it. He looked to be around Trip's age and was exactly Marcus's height, five eleven. He was wearing a dark blue T-shirt, shorts, and flip-flops. He introduced himself as Bob Abramson and showed Marcus in.

The cottage was sparsely furnished in typical summer style, and an open suitcase sat on the floor in the middle of the living room rug.

Bob offered Marcus coffee, which he declined; he was already too wound up. "Thanks for seeing me," he said as Bob offered him a chair. "I wonder if you'd mind telling me how long you knew Trip?" He'd decided that was the most bland, inoffensive way to start.

They had known each other for a few years, Bob said. They'd met here, in Miller's Cove, several summers ago, when they'd both just finished their first year of college, Trip at Harvard, Bob at Brown. Bob was from Connecticut.

"I hope you'll forgive me for asking if you were in a relationship with Trip. I only ask because his parents want to know if he was seeing someone. I guess he didn't share many personal details with his family. We gay men usually don't," Marcus said. He knew it was an awkward question, but he was hoping to establish some rapport that might yield a lead.

Bob ran a hand through his curls. "We dated a few times, but we didn't click as a couple."

"I know how that works," Marcus said with a bit of a chuckle.

Bob smiled and looked directly at Marcus for the first time. He'd lost touch with Trip, he said, but they'd run into each other a few months ago in Cambridge. Bob had been admitted to the Harvard Law School and was in town looking things over. Trip invited him to have lunch, and Bob mentioned that he'd rented a place in Miller's Cove for the summer. Trip jumped at the chance when he heard the house had a second bedroom and that Bob was looking for a roommate.

"So you're off to law school in the fall?"

"I decided to delay a year. I need a break."

Marcus nodded. "That's probably smart."

"We weren't having sex, not with each other, in case you're wondering," Bob offered without prompting. "Of course the police asked."

"Thanks for telling me that." Marcus paused. "Can you tell me about the day Trip died?"

"He cleaned the house—we took turns—and then headed for the beach. He was back in the early afternoon. I wasn't feeling great, so I hung around here and slept on

and off all day. He went out again around 5:30, said he was
going to grab something to eat and then meet someone for
a drink."

"Did he say who? Or where they were meeting?"

"No, I have no idea. I told the police."

Marcus frowned. The person Trip was meeting for a
drink might have been the murderer. Or not. The police
had said Trip was probably killed around 9:30, just as the
fireworks started. He might have had a drink with someone
and been murdered after that, by someone else.

"Was he dating anyone?"

"Trip didn't date. About twice a week he'd come home
with a guy from the Club or the beach, and they'd be hot and
heavy for a few days, and then that was that. On to the next."

Marcus was surprised. For one thing, they were in the
middle of the AIDS crisis, and there were no treatments.
Gay men were dying everywhere. And he'd imagined that
Trip would have been more interested in a real boyfriend, not
a steady stream of sex partners. Then again, Trip was young
and gorgeous, and there was a huge supply of potential
partners around Miller's Cove in the summer, men from
Canada and up and down the East Coast. It might have been
too much to resist.

If there had been a parade of men in and out of Trip's
bed, all of them could be murder suspects.

"The police wanted name, rank, and serial number for
all these guys," Bob went on, "but of course I had no idea
who any of them were. I might see them in the kitchen in the
morning for five minutes, but that was it. I gave the police
a first name or two, a few descriptions. I remembered one
guy from London pretty well, but there were so many, and I
didn't exactly keep notes."

There was an awkward silence as Marcus absorbed this information. Bob broke it by asking, "Would you like to see his room?"

It was a small room with a double bed, a small dresser, a tiny closet, and a large desk. On one side of the desk was a stack of folders labeled "Thesis." Marcus felt a pang. On the other side was a pile of newspapers and clippings, and he studied them carefully. The local paper was open to a story about a gay man being taunted by rowdy teenagers from Wells, a town down the road from Miller's Cove, but without its more cosmopolitan clientele. There were several clippings about a Boston politician named Frank Murphy, who was suspected of taking kickbacks from a construction company—standard Boston politics, Marcus knew—and some other clippings about a drug bust in Portland. There were also a few books at the back of the desk: Lincoln's speeches, two Lincoln biographies, and Deena Echols's book on nineteenth-century rhetoric, which Trip had used as a reference.

Bob hovered in the doorway.

Marcus looked quickly through the thesis folders. On top he found notes and drafts of various sections of the thesis, nothing out of the ordinary; it all tracked with the final product. There were a few drafts with Marcus's notes and corrections.

"He spent a lot of time at his desk," Bob said.

Marcus thought that was a bit odd; Trip had just graduated, he was on summer holiday in a beach town, and there wouldn't have been any reason to keep working on the thesis. Once a project like that was done, most students didn't want to think about the topic again, or anything else academic, at least for a while.

"Did you get any sense of why, or what he was doing at the desk?"

Bob considered for a moment. "He said one thing that seemed pretty strange, now that I think about it. He came into the living room late one night, really excited, and said, 'I've nailed it. It's all right there, in the papers.'"

Marcus looked back at the pile of newspapers. What was there? What had Trip found, or figured out? "Did you ask him what he meant?"

"No, it was really late, and I was half asleep, and Trip left the house right after that. I think he was meeting someone."

"Did you tell the police about this?"

"No, I just remembered it now. I was pretty nervous when the police were here. I think they see me as a suspect."

"That's only natural."

"I guess."

"You said it was late. Did Trip often go out late at night?"

"Well, yeah. The Club is open 'til two, and sometimes people hang around in the parking lot after that. Trip liked that scene."

Again Marcus found this picture of Trip jarring.

"I'm going to take some notes, if that's okay."

Marcus opened the desk drawer and pulled out a blank sheet of paper. The drawer's contents were unremarkable: pens, pencils, paper clips, rubber bands, and a few condoms. *At least he was safe; thank God for that*, Marcus thought.

"I assume the police told you not to touch any of this stuff?"

"No, they didn't. They took pictures, but that was all."

Marcus jotted down some brief notes about the newspaper articles: names, dates, a few details. Underneath the stories about Murphy were a few clippings about Sidney

Putnam, a Harvard chemistry professor accused of sexually harassing a male graduate student. Marcus knew about the case; it had been the talk of the campus for a while that spring.

"Would you do me a favor?" he asked Bob as he was leaving. "If you remember anything else, please contact me. I'm here for another two weeks, then back in Cambridge." Marcus wrote down both numbers on a scrap of paper.

He noticed the suitcase again and asked Bob where he was headed.

"Nowhere. I was supposed to be going to a cousin's wedding in Hartford, but I missed it. I guess I'm a murder suspect."

"I wouldn't worry. The police automatically consider a roommate a suspect. I'm sure you'll be in the clear soon."

They shook hands. Bob seemed to stare at Marcus as he said good-bye, and held on to his hand longer than necessary.

"Thanks again, Bob. Sorry to have bothered you. And try not to worry about the police."

"No bother. I hope someone can find the killer. Trip didn't deserve this, even if he was a bit of a slut."

7

It's all right there, in the papers.

What was Trip up to? Amateur journalism? Real journalism? Was he planning to write an article and sell it to the Boston papers? During one of their thesis sessions that spring, Trip had said he thought it would be fun to be an investigative reporter. Maybe he'd been planning to start with a local story and work in journalism for a while before heading to law school or business school or whatever golden future his background guaranteed him.

It's all right there, in the papers.

Clearly it was a lead. Or was it a red herring? Maybe the murder was a simple story, a disgruntled boyfriend killing Trip in a jealous rage, a robbery gone wrong. Marcus could easily imagine both, especially now that he knew more about Trip's habits—lots of partners, lots of late nights.

Back at the inn, Marcus put on his swim trunks, took a quick dip in the pool, then sat in a deck chair with his notes from Trip's desk.

The police would follow up on the locals, the boyfriends, if you could call them that, and any other leads in Miller's

Cove. He didn't need to cover that angle, and they would be angry if he impeded their investigation. They would also notify the Harvard authorities and the Cambridge police, who would look into Trip's life there. No need to cover that ground either.

What the police didn't know was what Marcus had just heard from Bob—that Trip had found something, some kind of lead to . . . what? Might Trip have stuck his nose too far into someone's business? It was a possibility.

Marcus wondered for a moment if he should share his information with the police but decided against it. If he did, they'd tell him to stay out of it.

But he was in. He realized with a start that he was all in. He had crossed a line, he was going to do this. If he found a lead of real substance, he would report it to Fitzgerald. Until then, he would just make discreet inquiries as a friend of the family.

No harm, no foul.

He called Kennebunkport again. David answered, and Marcus asked him for a picture of Trip he could show around where necessary. David dropped it off later that day while Marcus was in the shower. It was in a heavy cream-colored envelope with a watermark and an address tastefully printed on the back: 14 Louisburg Square, Boston. The desk clerk said David had looked quite nervous when he dropped off the envelope, and had whiskey on his breath. Marcus explained that his brother was the victim of the recent murder.

Louisburg Square. Of course. The toniest address in the city, a privately owned square on Beacon Hill, surrounded by stately townhouses where Boston society's crème de la crème had resided since early in the nineteenth century. The painter John Singleton Copley had lived there; Louisa May Alcott had died there. The famous opera singer Jenny Lind was married in one of the square's parlors. Senator John Kerry and his wife lived there now, when they weren't in Washington or at one of their numerous other properties. No doubt the Howard townhouse had been renovated and came complete with elevator, servant's quarters on the lower level, and priceless antiques and paintings.

On Christmas Eve every year, by tradition, Louisburg Square was visited by carolers, and some of the bluebloods opened their parlors to strangers. Marcus had gone one year to listen to the carolers and watch, had seen the open doors but hadn't ventured inside. As he thought about it, he realized that was how he felt at Harvard—peering in from outside. And it was how he felt now, with Trip's family. Not a friend, not an equal, not an employee. In between.

Peering in.

The picture David had left nearly brought tears to Marcus's eyes. Trip was casually dressed, smiling his perfect smile, looking like someone had just told him the funniest joke in the world. He was standing on the steps of the Beacon Hill townhouse, wearing a light jacket with the collar turned up. It was autumn, there were orange and gold leaves on the trees. It was a perfectly composed photo, almost professional. A perfect photo of a perfect young man in a perfect setting.

Except he wasn't going to have a perfect life, the life to which the accident of his birth made him entitled.

Marcus put the photo back in its envelope, looked over his notes, and decided on his next move.

8

After grabbing a sandwich at the deli, Marcus headed over to what Bob had called The Club, the only gay disco in town. He had stuck his head in the night after he arrived in Miller's Cove, but most of the gyrating bodies were in their early twenties, the music was too loud, and it wasn't his scene at all. Not that he really had a scene. His forays into gay discos were always brief and increasingly rare. He was never comfortable in the dance clubs and thought they were silly places to try to meet someone, since everyone was drinking and you couldn't talk over the music. He met people mostly through friends and the occasional meeting of the few gay or liberal organizations he followed, the National Gay and Lesbian Task Force, the ACLU. He had never been a disco bunny, even when he first came out in college. He hated disco music.

The Club door was open. Handsome young staffers were mopping up from the night before, getting things ready for that evening. He asked one of them for the manager and was directed to a small office at the back with a door marked "Private." It was slightly ajar. He knocked and heard "Come in."

A very tall man sat at a large desk shuffling papers.

He was gaudily dressed in a flowered shirt and too much jewelry—a gold chain around his neck, gold bracelet, a gold pinky ring. He was fortyish, and it looked like he'd had a hair transplant and a facelift. There was a nameplate on the desk: Dan Carter.

Marcus introduced himself and they shook hands. Marcus explained that he'd known the recent murder victim and had been asked by his family to look into things. He wasn't sure how else to account for his presence there. He showed Carter the picture.

"Yeah, horrible thing," Carter said with a heavy Brooklyn accent. "Cops already been here. I recognize the kid. He was a regular. He was hot, got lots of attention. It's a shame. And terrible for business."

"Did you ever speak to him?" Marcus tried to hide that he was taken aback by a murder being described as bad for business.

"No."

"Do you know if any of your employees did?"

Carter hesitated. "Maybe Joe, one of the bartenders. He'll be here at five."

It was 2:30. Marcus thanked Carter and said he'd be back. He returned to the inn, took a swim and a nap, and woke just in time for Joe's shift.

A strapping, gorgeous hunk was behind the bar, wiping it down. He was wearing a blue muscle shirt that matched his eyes and left nothing to the imagination. He had a short, military haircut. *That had to be good for business*, Marcus thought, *men must buy more drinks just to get a closer look.*

"Are you Joe?"

"Might be. Who wants to know?"

Marcus introduced himself, showed Joe the picture, and

explained what he was doing.

"Poor kid. Yeah, I talked to him a few times. We even made out one night in back while I was on a break."

"You made out?"

"Yeah, but that was all. I didn't tell the police about it. It's none of their fucking business."

"Can you tell me anything that might be relevant? His family is really hurting."

Joe hesitated for a long time, staring at Marcus, then resumed wiping down the bar. "He liked G."

G was GHB, a club drug becoming popular in the gay community. It was said to produce feelings of euphoria, at least for a while.

Marcus was startled, and Joe could see that.

"I know. Rich kid like that, hot bod, you figure he's got it made. He don't need drugs."

"Do you have any idea where he got it?"

Joe hesitated again. "You sure you're not police or DEA?"

"No, no. Just a family friend, I swear. This is totally off the record."

"There's a guy from Portland who comes in about once a week, sells it out in the parking lot. His name is Smith, or so he says. He's usually here Friday nights late. He's around thirty, always wears a leather jacket, has a thick handlebar mustache. Easy to spot."

Marcus thanked him for the information and left The Club. He went back to the inn and called Bob, who asked if there was any news.

"No, not yet."

Marcus decided to plunge in. "Did you know Trip took G?"

There was a pause, and Bob seemed suddenly tense. "He never said, but he'd come home sometimes and it was pretty obvious he was on something, if not G then something like it."

"Could you do me a favor? Look at that article on the desk about the drug bust in Portland, see if it mentions G."

Bob came back to the phone in a couple of minutes. "It doesn't mention any specific drugs. Do you think there's some connection to Trip?"

"I don't know, but thanks."

Marcus hung up and went out to the pool deck to think. Why would a drug dealer kill a customer? For owing him money. But Trip had money, Marcus assumed, plenty of it. It didn't make sense, but he would follow up.

He had dinner at Maineium's again, opting for a hamburger, then went across the street to the Veranda, a popular piano bar. He ordered a glass of white wine, sat at a table, and listened to the piano player belt out show tunes. Everyone was in a good mood, probably a little tipsy. Or very tipsy.

It was Thursday evening. Marcus finished his wine, which gave him a pleasant buzz, and went back to the inn, where he fell into a deep, dreamless sleep.

9

On Friday morning, Marcus walked to the beach. He couldn't bring himself to sit in the shade under the awning, where Trip's body had been found, but others were sitting there, laughing, reading, doing the things people do on vacation, as if nothing had happened. The police had already removed the yellow tape. Marcus rented a beach chair from the hotel and sat on the sand in Section B, just listening to the waves.

He stayed well past lunch, knowing the main business of the day would be to show up at The Club late that night. When his stomach grumbled, he walked to a little chowder house halfway back to town, ordered vegetarian stew, and went back to the inn. He took a dip in the pool to wash off the sweat and sand from the beach, then took a nap. This napping was becoming a habit, he realized. Must be the sea air.

Marcus woke up around six and read a few pages of Emerson, but his mind was elsewhere. Why on earth would Trip go in for drugs and promiscuity? Just sowing wild oats? Was it only a summer thing? He was such a good student during the school year that he couldn't have been doing drugs or Marcus would surely have noticed something. Was there some psychological explanation, some emptiness inside that needed filling?

Marcus could well imagine that growing up on Louisburg Square, going to prep school, and summering in Kennebunkport were difficult propositions for a young gay man. Did Trip feel guilty, as if he were letting down the family and all that crap? Marcus remembered his own childhood, his own friends, and reminded himself that it wasn't just Yankees who expected rectitude. Most cultures did, most religions, as they had for thousands of years. Marcus could still see the pained look on his own parents' faces when he told them he was gay. They didn't scream or shout or throw him out, but he knew. He knew he was a disappointment, the kind of disappointment that a PhD from Princeton and a job at Harvard couldn't erase. Luckily he had two older siblings who married young and produced grandchildren. He wasn't sure the marriages were completely happy, but they were intact, and followed the well-established script.

Marcus had a late dinner at Maineium's, then went to the Veranda, which was busy with a weekend crowd and louder than usual. He ordered Poland Spring, Maine's sparkling water, because he wanted his wits about him when he talked to the drug dealer. A single guy struck up a conversation, and Marcus was polite but not interested. The Veranda got cruisy on weekends.

Around 11:00 he went back to the inn and changed clothes, hoping to look like someone who wasn't out of place in a disco at midnight. He put on a dark blue T-shirt and jeans, the best he could manage.

"What the hell am I doing?" he muttered under his breath as he walked toward The Club. He was looking for a drug dealer in the dead of night, but to ask him what?

Marcus tried to calm himself down, told himself there would be lots of people around and he was in no real danger.

There was no one matching the dealer's description in the parking lot when Marcus got there, so he loitered inside The Club for a while. The place was packed. There were so many granite bodies dancing that there was hardly any air, so after a while Marcus went back to the parking lot, where lots was going on: couples kissing, pressing against each other, a few guys smoking cigarettes, a group of three loud and boisterous.

At the edge of the lot he saw someone fitting the description he had been given and walked in that direction.

"Are you Smith?" Marcus asked.

"Might be. Who wants to know?"

Do these guys rehearse their lines together?

"Look," Marcus said, and Smith immediately tensed up. "I'm not a cop. I'm not law enforcement. I'm not here to give you any trouble, but you probably heard a young guy was killed in town a few nights ago. I'm trying to find out what happened. His family asked me to."

Smith scowled. "Why should I believe you?"

"Because he was a friend, and I cared about him."

"Just a friend? He wasn't your bitch?"

"No!" Marcus snapped, and produced Trip's photo. He was getting angry. It was time to play the Ivy League card, though he wasn't sure it would have any effect on a drug dealer. "I am a professor at Harvard, and this young man was my student. He was brilliant, with his whole life ahead of him, and I'm going to find out what happened to him."

Marcus clenched his fists. He hoped he was coming across like a tough cop, someone like Lieutenant Samuels on *Cagney & Lacey*, one of the few TV shows Marcus watched regularly.

"Okay, professor, okay," Smith said, his eyes softening slightly as he looked at Trip's buoyant smile. "Okay, yeah, he was a customer. Not a regular, but every once in a while he'd buy weed."

"What about G?"

Smith thought. "No, I never sold him G."

"Are you sure?"

"Yeah, I'm sure. Weed a couple of times. That's it."

"And he paid you right away?"

"Yeah, cash. Only way I operate."

Marcus thanked him and strode off, grateful not to have been beaten up or worse. His heart was racing and he was sweating.

Safely back at the inn, he sat outside in a deck chair. There were a couple of possibilities. Smith could have been lying or just not remembering. Or the bartender could have gotten things wrong. Or Trip got the G from someone else, didn't buy it himself. Or Bob Abramson could have been wrong—maybe Trip was just high on weed, not G. Weed made most people mellow, Marcus knew—hell, it made him mellow the few times he smoked it in Ann Arbor, but everyone was different. Some people got giggly on weed. Maybe that's what Bob had seen those nights when Trip came home late. But whatever he was taking, if he paid cash, then a drug dealer as the murderer just didn't make any sense.

Dead end, Marcus thought as he dragged himself inside and up the stairs to bed. "Fresh start tomorrow, Waldo," he said to the Emerson volume lying unopened on the dresser.

10

The morning was cool, and Marcus woke late. He got downstairs just in time to snag a bagel before the breakfast things were put away, then sat on the deck in his cotton sweater with a cup of coffee. Around 11:00 the inn owner's cute boyfriend came out and told him he had a phone call.

It was David Howard, wondering if Marcus needed anything.

"Not really, but I do have a question that might help me piece things together. What kind of access to funds did Trip have?"

There was a long pause, and Marcus suspected that the question felt intrusive. In families like that, one never spoke of money, certainly not to outsiders.

There was some tension in David's voice. "Trip came into a trust at twenty-one," David said finally. "It provided a steady monthly income, quite generous. It would have increased at age thirty, and then again at forty. I have the same arrangement. Of course the family paid his Harvard expenses."

"So as far as you know, Trip never had financial problems?"

"No. It was a generous trust. When he turned twenty-one, Trip spent the summer in Europe, came home, and bought a sports car. Why do you ask?"

"Just wondered. I'm trying to get as complete a picture of his life as I can. Might help me think of an avenue to explore. One more question. Was Trip working as a journalist or writing freelance articles?"

"Not that I know of. Why?"

"There were a bunch of newspaper stories on his desk in the house he was sharing, but they weren't about anything I thought would interest him."

"I see." There was another pause. "Be sure to let us know if you need anything."

Marcus went upstairs to retrieve his notes from the newspapers on Trip's desk. Could Trip have been looking into the stories about Murphy, the Boston pol who was suspected of taking kickbacks?

Maybe Bob Abramson had remembered something else that might be useful by now. Marcus went inside, called him, and invited him to lunch.

They met at Maineium's. This time Bob was wearing a polo shirt, pleated shorts, and sandals, and had had a haircut and combed his hair. Marcus realized with a start that he was incredibly good looking; he hadn't really noticed before.

They made small talk, and then Marcus brought up the newspaper clippings.

"Did Trip ever mention that he was working as a journalist, or trying to? Or mention a corrupt Boston politician or a Harvard chemistry professor?"

Bob thought for a moment. "He told me once about a chemistry professor he'd run into at a gay bar in Boston."

"Oh?"

"Yeah. Trip said this guy hit on him but he wasn't interested. I think Trip only went for younger guys."

That might be important information. Could the chemistry professor have been obsessed with Trip? It wasn't hard to imagine, but obsessed enough to kill?

"Did he ever mention the professor's name?"

Bob said he hadn't. "Are you getting anywhere?"

"No, not really," Marcus said as their food arrived. As they ate, Bob asked Marcus about himself, where he was from, what he taught, what he did for fun.

"Fun?" Marcus laughed. "Junior professors aren't supposed to have fun. We're supposed to work eighteen hours a day."

"Well," Bob replied with a sly smile, "you're here, aren't you?"

The talk turned to movies, the lingua franca of American life, and Marcus could see that Bob was an insightful, bright young man. He had written a senior honors thesis at Brown on Southern women in film, starting with Bette Davis in *Jezebel* and, of course, Vivien Leigh, and his comments were quite smart. For a moment Marcus got the sense that Bob was flirting with him, but he quickly put the notion out of his head. I'm too old for him, he told himself.

And he's a suspect. Sort of. And I'm imagining things. Wishful thinking.

After lunch they wandered around a bit. Bob seemed in no hurry to leave. He asked Marcus where he was staying. Marcus pointed to the inn on the hill.

"I hear they have a nice pool," he said.

"Yes, it's very nice."

"I have a bathing suit on under my shorts." Bob grinned. Marcus was startled. "Would you like to take a dip?"

What else could he say?

They walked to the inn and went to Marcus's room. Bob stripped down to his suit and Marcus put on his, trying not to look at Bob but catching sight of his smooth, strong back. Granite chest too, Marcus saw. At the pool Bob dove in while Marcus sat in a chair under an umbrella. Bob was an excellent swimmer, swift and steady. Beautiful.

After more laps than Marcus could count, Bob climbed out of the water and joined him under the umbrella. Marcus handed him a towel.

"Great pool, perfect temperature," Bob said. He looked relaxed.

They chatted about the inn. Bob started to make up stories about the other guests lounging around them.

"That one is married to a woman, but he's a closet case. He told his wife in Newton he had a business meeting in Portland." Newton was a suburb of Boston.

"And that couple is trying to work things out. It's not going well." It was a gay couple from D.C., Marcus knew, and it was true, they had the look of people who were together but not happily.

Marcus fetched them glasses of iced tea from the guest kitchen. They sat comfortably, and after a while Bob said that he should be getting home. As they said their good-byes, Bob leaned over and kissed Marcus on the cheek.

"Thanks for the swim, and for lunch. Why don't you come over for dinner tomorrow night?" he said as Marcus walked him through the inn onto the deck that led down to the street. "Around seven o'clock? I'll cook."

Marcus didn't have to think before he agreed. He suddenly felt happy for the first time since he'd heard about Trip's death.

11

Marcus spent the evening reading in his room on and off, in between thinking about Bob and thinking about Trip. He realized there was little more he could do in Miller's Cove and that he'd need to go back to Cambridge if he wanted to pursue the leads from Trip's room. He'd have dinner with Bob tomorrow and leave the following day.

He spent the next morning on the pool deck, then walked down to the beach. He still wasn't ready to sit under the awning, even though he really craved the shade, so he rented a beach chair again, walked down to Section B, and read Emerson, able to concentrate on something other than the murder for the first time in a while. In the late afternoon he walked back to the inn and took another nap.

Around six he showered and dressed. He stopped for a bottle of good wine on his way to Bob's house and knocked just after seven.

Bob opened the door with a big smile and kissed Marcus on the cheek. He smelled great. Marcus could also smell something good coming from the kitchen, and he sat at the small kitchen table while Bob finished cooking, chatting away. The table had been set carefully, with a tablecloth and a candle, which Bob lit before he served the food.

He had made a quiche and an abundant salad with blue cheese and pears. He had baked a loaf of sourdough bread, which was still warm from the oven and delicious. For dessert he'd made a sponge cake.

"My Bubbe's recipe," he said as he poured Marcus a cup of strong black coffee. "You probably don't know what a Bubbe is, do you?" Bob asked, laughing.

"Of course I do. I had two. Although I only knew one. She baked too."

"You're Jewish?" Bob was incredulous. "I don't believe it."

"Born and raised. I had a Bar Mitzvah. 'Baruch atah Adonai . . .'"

"George doesn't strike me as a Jewish name. I assumed you were Catholic. Or something."

"Ellis Island. The name was Gourevitch, but the immigration officer couldn't pronounce it. Or spell it. So he changed it."

The cake was delicious, and the conversation flowed: Miller's Cove, Harvard, news about the Unabomber and the new compact discs, Bob's future as a lawyer. He wanted to practice environmental law, or possibly intellectual property.

After dinner they sat on the front porch. It was a pleasant, cool evening, and Marcus felt relaxed. They continued to talk but were also comfortable with silence as they finished the bottle of wine. After a while Marcus thanked Bob for dinner and got up to leave.

"Um, why don't you stay," Bob said after a brief hesitation.

Marcus couldn't have been more shocked if he had said, "I murdered Trip." He gulped.

"Are you sure?"

"Yes."

"We'll have to be careful." It was 1985.

Bob smiled. "Of course." He stood up and kissed Marcus, on the lips this time, then took him by the hand.

12

The next morning, they took a shower together, splashing and laughing, and headed to Maineium's for a late breakfast. Bob asked Marcus what he was going to do the rest of the day.

"I really should go back to town, follow up on those articles Trip had on his desk. There's nothing more I can do here. The Miller's Cove police will be following up any local leads."

"Yeah, they are. I've heard from a bunch of people that they're asking about Trip all over town. Everyone is scared, and the police have increased patrols. All the merchants are worried about the effect on business."

"I really should drive back to Cambridge, but I don't want to leave," Marcus hastened to add.

Bob looked relieved. "Invite me down. It's a short drive, I can come for an evening. If you want me to."

"Of course I want you to," Marcus said. He could hardly remember wanting anything quite so much.

Bob flashed that smile of his. He was young enough that he looked absolutely gorgeous after their night of exertions, while Marcus was sure he had dark circles under his eyes and looked like a vagabond.

After breakfast they kissed good-bye on the street; this was a gay resort, after all. Marcus gave Bob his address in Cambridge, phone number, and directions.

Marcus returned to the inn. He had about twelve days left on his reservation, and he knew he wouldn't get a refund if he checked out early. He decided to keep the room in case he needed to come back to Miller's Cove to work on Trip's case. Or to see Bob. They could use the pool.

He packed his bag and was on the way to his car when the innkeeper caught him at the front door and asked what was up. Marcus said an emergency had called him back to town but he'd be back before his reservation ended.

His apartment on Kirkland Street, which he rented from the University, was hot and a bit musty when he got there. It had a large living room, a kitchen, and a bedroom with a little alcove where Marcus had installed his desk, the one good piece of furniture he'd bought when he moved in. The building was from the 1940s, solidly constructed, and had fine wood doors with glass handles. The walls were thick and Marcus hardly ever heard his neighbors, who pretty much kept to themselves, assistant professors and staff members mostly, and the occasional pair of married graduate students.

Marcus opened the windows, turned on the ceiling fan in the living room, made some iced tea from a mix, and unpacked. He went to the corner grocery store to pick up a few things, including dark chocolate—Bob had said he loved dark chocolate—then sat at this desk to decide on next steps. He ate two pieces of the chocolate.

There were two leads to follow up: Murphy, the corrupt politician, and Sidney Putnam, the chemistry professor. Marcus wasn't sure how to go about investigating either, but he decided the chemistry professor would be easier to tackle.

He had a friend on the faculty, a biologist named Darren Jones, who would know about what was going on at Harvard in the sciences. Marcus called him and invited him to lunch the next day. He yawned and gave in to his new nap habit, and when he got up ordered pizza for dinner.

He'd never really learned how to cook.

In the morning, he wired flowers to Bob, worked a bit on Emerson, then headed to Harvard Square to meet Darren at the same restaurant where he'd had lunch with Trip. He felt a stab of sadness as he greeted his friend and sat down. They caught up, the usual chitchat, and then Marcus asked if Darren knew Sidney Putnam.

"I've met him, seen him at a few parties, we've talked about each other's work. We've shared some graduate students. Don't know him well."

"Do you think he harassed that student?"

"I have no idea. You never really know about someone's sex life, do you?"

Marcus laughed. "No, you certainly don't."

As they were finishing their meals, Darren mentioned that there was a party coming up, a sendoff for someone going to Oxford for a year, and that Putnam would probably be there.

"Can you invite me?" Marcus asked.

"I suppose. It's an informal party, and I'm sure people will just show up, but why are you so interested in meeting Putnam?"

"Very long story," Marcus said. He got the details and thanked Darren.

The party was a few nights away, on a Friday. Marcus went to his office at Holyoke Center, sorted through the accumulated mail, then went back to his apartment and called

Bob and invited him down for the weekend. Bob thanked him for the flowers and said he'd be there Friday.

"Anything happening in Miller's Cove?" Marcus asked.

"Just the usual, Speedos and suntan lotion."

Marcus spent the time before Bob arrived working on Emerson. It went well, he made useful notes and was able to concentrate. It was amazing what sex did for the mind, he realized. He also did a bit of research at Widener on the Howard family, and was amazed to find out how blue their blood really was. The family could trace its roots to the eleventh century in England.

Bob arrived Friday afternoon and they tumbled into bed, laughing. When they woke, they had a quick dinner of tuna fish sandwiches, then headed to the party. Marcus explained why they were going. "One of us should try to get into a conversation with Putnam and mention Trip," he told Bob, "see how he reacts."

"Does this make me Watson to your Sherlock?" Bob teased as they walked the short distance to the address Marcus had been given.

"Well, I'm not sure they ever had sex," Marcus said.

"No, Holmes was all in his head. Probably no sex ever. Total closet case."

The party was in a private home on Irving Street. They found the front door open and walked in to find a large crowd. It was one of those cavernous old Cambridge houses and it belonged to the chair of the chemistry department, who greeted them near the door and pretended to know who they were.

Marcus quickly located his friend Darren, introduced Bob, and fetched drinks for all three of them, white wine in plastic cups.

"Which one is Putnam?" Marcus asked.

Darren pointed to a man standing in a corner holding forth, surrounded by graduate students.

"Why don't you sidle over, be flirty, see what happens," Marcus whispered to Bob.

Bob smirked. "Right, Sherlock."

Putnam noticed Bob right away. They shook hands as Bob introduced himself. Putnam was tall, distinguished-looking, around fifty, and wearing what looked to be a very expensive linen suit in a color that could only be called taupe. Everyone in the little group surrounding him chatted away, but Putnam clearly had an eye for Bob.

After a while Bob extracted himself and rejoined Marcus.

"Anything?" Marcus asked.

"Nothing. I mentioned Trip, the murder, and that Trip had just graduated. I asked Putnam point blank if he knew him. Nothing. He didn't blink. No reaction at all. I think he really didn't know him."

"Well, thanks for trying."

"He did ask me to meet him later, but I said I was recovering from the clap."

Marcus choked on his wine.

They stayed for a while so as not to arouse suspicion, listening to snatches of conversation about DNA which neither of them understood, then said good-bye to Darren and walked back to Kirkland Street. The party host gave them a puzzled look as they departed.

It was a lovely night with a cool breeze. "Gee, I wonder what we should do now," Bob said as they walked.

"Come upstairs and I'll show you. That is, if you don't have the clap."

Bob threw back his head and arched his eyebrows. "I'm

not that kind of girl."

"Oh yes you are," Marcus said, grabbing him around the waist. He was beginning to wonder who he was, grabbing a boyfriend on the street and crashing parties.

13

He woke to the smell of coffee and eggs frying in the kitchen. He kissed Bob on the cheek and reached for the orange juice.

"What next?" Bob asked. "That is, after you explain to me the organizing principle you use in this kitchen."

Marcus chuckled. "The uncertainty principle. Let's go back to the beach. The weather's supposed to be great."

They ate, packed up, and were back at Bob's by noon. After changing, they stopped for sandwiches and headed for Section B of the beach. Marcus dozed over his Emerson volume while Bob swam, seemingly oblivious to the temperature of the water.

In the late afternoon they napped in Marcus's room at the inn, Bob's head resting on Marcus's shoulder. Marcus watched Bob's sleeping face for a while, wondering what Bob saw in him. Then he thought of something he'd once said to a Harvard student who had had a stroke of unexpected good fortune. "You know, Sam, I went to the University of Michigan, and I went to football games. At the time, it was the largest outdoor stadium in the world. And this is what I learned: When the ball lands in your arms, don't ask questions. Run."

Marcus smiled and kissed Bob on the forehead.

In the evening Bob went back to his house to change, and they met at the Veranda for a drink. They ate at an Italian place, lingering over dessert and coffee. Then Bob wanted go to The Club.

"Come on, I want to show you off," he teased.

"Okay, okay."

Bob pulled Marcus onto the dance floor when the DJ played the Pointer Sisters. For the first time in his life, Marcus enjoyed dancing. Bob danced with such grace that Marcus was transfixed. He followed Bob's moves, sweat pouring down from both of them. They were completely in sync.

The next day they woke to gentle rain. Bob went out early to get the newspapers and lox and bagels, and they lounged around all morning. The local paper carried a short follow-up story about Trip's murder, saying the police were still investigating, giving no details.

All afternoon they cuddled and napped. For dinner they ordered takeout from a local grill, and Bob made a salad while Marcus picked it up. The rain stopped and started.

The next morning at breakfast Bob was unusually subdued.

"Marcus, there's something I should tell you."

Marcus put his coffee cup down.

"Trip did take G. In fact I did it too, just once, but Trip did a lot of it."

Marcus was surprised but tried not to show it.

"It was the beginning of the summer. Trip had just moved in, and someone he knew invited us to a party. It was at a big house at the edge of town, owned by this rich gay couple from New York. One of them worked in theater. There were pretty people there from all over, including a few actors, and the hosts passed around a lot of drugs—coke, weed, G."

Bob got up and poured more coffee. He was clearly upset.

"At first I said no, but Trip really pushed me, and I thought, what the hell, try it. It didn't have much of an effect on me at all, but Trip seemed to love it."

Bob sat back down. "Trip started hanging out with those guys a lot. In fact he stayed over there a few times, and I think maybe he slept with one of them, but who knows. He got lots of G from them."

Marcus put his hand on top of Bob's. "Thanks for telling me."

"I didn't tell you at first because I didn't want you to think I was some kind of druggie. And I don't even know why I did it that night. I wasn't comfortable with that crowd, I guess I was just nervous."

"I can understand that. I'm like that at parties too."

"Yeah, but I'll bet you never did G."

"Well, no, but I sometimes drink more than I should."

Bob tried to smile. "It's just that I wanted to impress you. I didn't want you to think I was an airhead."

Marcus was touched. "Trust me, I never thought that. Except when you went on a bit too long about Bette Davis."

That made both of them laugh.

They were both standing now, clearing the table. Marcus put his arms around Bob and hugged him tight. "I'll tell Fitzgerald about the couple. Do you think there could be any connection to Trip's murder?"

Bob considered for a moment. "I don't think so. It was just a bit of summer fun. For all of them. They were rich, Trip was hot, what would be the motive?"

Marcus could think of a few—jealousy, for instance, perhaps Trip sleeping with one of them and the other the jealous murderer—but he didn't want to prolong the conversation and Bob's distress.

"I'm sorry I lied to you. Really sorry," Bob said.

"It's okay. Really. But I'm glad you told me. Everyone lies sometimes. If you asked me my weight, I'd knock off five pounds."

Bob exhaled as if he'd been holding his breath for the last five minutes. Marcus could almost see him shifting gears.

"Okay, Sherlock, so what's the next step?"

"I have to explore the corrupt politician, somehow," Marcus said.

"Maybe start with the reporter who broke the story," Bob suggested.

"That's a good idea."

"Elementary, my dear Sherlock."

Marcus laughed, then went into Trip's room, pulled out the newspaper clipping, and wrote down the reporter's name: John Simmons of *The Boston Globe*.

After breakfast Marcus drove back to town. They agreed Bob would come down on Wednesday and they'd come back to Miller's Cove for the weekend.

When he got back to Kirkland Street Marcus ate some yogurt, then called Fitzgerald and told him about the gay couple.

Fitzgerald said the police had already checked them out and they were clean. "In fact, they were in Los Angeles over the Fourth, and there was no motive. Trip had sex with both of them, which apparently was routine for the couple. It all checked out. We didn't even bust them for the drugs. The local merchants want us to look the other way, or else some of the rich summer crowd would stay away."

Marcus was relieved that the story ended.

Marcus then called the *Globe* and asked for John Simmons. He wasn't at his desk, so Marcus left his name and number on voicemail. The reporter called back an hour later.

Marcus gave him a vague account of why he was calling and asked if they could meet for coffee or a drink. Simmons said he was free around 6:30 and suggested the Bull and Finch, a pub on Beacon Street that within a few years would become the setting for the television series *Cheers*. It was owned by a former baseball player for the Red Sox, like the character in the series. Before the series it was a comfortable neighborhood place that served the best hamburgers in the city.

Marcus found Simmons waiting for him, sipping a Sam Adams. He ordered a Coors Light for himself and explained his connection with the Howard family and his discovery of Simmons's article about Frank Murphy among Trip's things.

Simmons took a swig of beer. "Terrible thing, that murder," he said.

Marcus agreed, and told Simmons a bit about Trip's academic record. He asked if Trip had contacted him.

"Yes, he did. He said his brother David was on the legislative committee that had oversight of state construction projects, and suggested I speak to him."

"And did you contact David Howard?"

"I did. I interviewed him in his office. He spoke strictly off the record. He gave me some background about the project and about Murphy's role on the Boston City Council."

Marcus wondered why David hadn't mentioned that. "Anything else?"

"David played his cards close to his chest. He wouldn't

say whether he thought Murphy was guilty. He seemed quite nervous."

"Hmm," Marcus murmured.

Simmons asked if Marcus was finding anything about Trip's murder.

"Off the record, no. Dead ends so far."

"It's a jarring story," Simmons said, "and public interest is high. Harvard golden boy, very prominent family, murdered in a gay resort. We ran the story and one brief follow-up."

They talked a bit more about nothing in particular, and Simmons took his leave. Marcus thanked him for his help.

After he had gone, Marcus walked across the street to the Public Garden, which was in full bloom and glorious in the twilight. He paused at the statue of George Washington—which made George look much slimmer than he was in real life—then crossed the street in front of the entrance of the Ritz Hotel, where kings and queens and presidents had stayed. He walked down Newbury Street and stopped at a soup and salad place for dinner.

Nothing was adding up. Frank Murphy presumably knew nothing about Trip. But why would David be nervous talking about it?

After his salad he bought himself a gelato, then walked to Copley Square and stared for a moment at the Boston Public Library, which he had explored when he first arrived in the city. The building was lavishly decorated and had a children's room, the first of its kind, and a central courtyard. It was a beautiful spot, and Marcus had enjoyed just sitting in the main reading room, imagining the literary figures and book lovers who had been there before him, stretching back to before the Civil War.

He left the library, hopped on the T—Boston's subway—

and headed back to Kirkland Street. When he got there, he telephoned David Howard and asked if they could meet. David said he'd be back in Boston tomorrow and that they could meet in the afternoon.

He then called Bob, asked how he had spent his day, and felt happy just to hear his voice. They talked for a long time, about everything, and nothing.

The next morning Marcus went to his wire cage at Widener Library to work and check out some books, then went back to his apartment and had a peanut butter sandwich for lunch.

I really need to eat better, he told himself. And learn how to cook.

14

The capitol building of the Commonwealth of Massachusetts sits at the crest of Beacon Hill and is considered one of the most beautiful buildings in America. It was designed by Charles Bulfinch and completed in 1798. Its original wood dome leaked and was covered in copper by Paul Revere's company in 1802. The interior was expanded and renovated several times, always in keeping with the original architecture. After the Civil War the copper was replaced by gold leaf. During World War II the gold got a coat of gray paint in case of air raids or attacks; after the war the gold was restored. Gleaming in the sun, it reminded everyone of John Winthrop's prescient phrase, a shining city on a hill, a phrase Ronald Reagan had recently used in a speech. You saw the Statehouse immediately as the T's Red Line exited its tunnel in Cambridge and crossed the Longfellow Bridge over the Charles River.

David Howard had asked Marcus to meet him on the steps leading to the main entrance of the Statehouse; he said he'd be finishing a meeting with the governor. Had he set it up that way to impress, Marcus wondered?

Marcus looked out from the steps to the Boston Common

across the street. The Common dated from 1634 and was the oldest public park in the United States. It was once used for grazing cows. Now, on this fine summer day, it was full of people strolling, lounging, talking, eating ice cream. Marcus wondered if ice cream had been part of John Winthrop's original plan for the colony. That made him smile.

David emerged just after 2:30 carrying several folders. He shook Marcus's hand and suggested they sit on one of the benches lining the Common. Marcus glanced at the folders as they walked. Something was nagging at him, just out of reach.

"So. Are you finding anything?" David asked.

"I'm afraid not much so far. I've followed up a few leads, but they've all proven to be dead ends. I do have a question for you though, related to one of the leads."

"By all means."

"In Trip's room in Miller's Cove, I found some clippings about a corruption scandal here in Boston involving the construction industry."

David's expression changed from friendly to neutral as Marcus went on.

"I wondered about Trip's interest, so I contacted the reporter at the *Globe* who wrote most of the stories. He said Trip had called him and suggested he speak to you."

"Yes, Trip did, and I did speak to the reporter. Simon, is that his name?"

"Simmons." Marcus suspected that David knew the real name but didn't want to say so.

"Right, Simmons. I couldn't tell him much. The oversight committee's investigation was ongoing. Still is. It's confidential, of course, at least until we have firm evidence of a crime. In absolute confidence, we don't have that yet. I doubt at this point that we will, even though I'm sure Murphy is crooked."

"I see. And as far as you know, Trip's only involvement was to refer the reporter to you?"

"As far as I know. Trip called me, asked me about the case, but again, I couldn't really discuss the details. Trip understood that. More or less. He pressed pretty hard, but that was his way."

"Did his interest in the case seem out of the ordinary?"

"It seemed intense, but I wouldn't say it set off any alarm bells. Trip could be a bit of a Boy Scout about local government, cared a lot about corruption, scandals, that sort of thing. He would get exercised. I had a feeling he'd end up a crusading lawyer some day," David said wistfully.

Marcus thought for a long moment. As David waited for Marcus to continue, he seemed to grow tense, and Marcus wondered why.

"I do have one more question," Marcus finally said. I hope you don't mind."

"Please." David checked his Rolex.

"You told me Trip had a trust fund. What happens to that money now that he's gone?"

David fiddled with the sleeves of his expensive suit. "Actually, it goes to me. The trust was established by our grandparents, and it's set up to benefit each generation of the family by a certain amount, however many children there might be." He paused, looked away.

"Of course I understand that makes me a suspect," he continued. "The police thought the same thing. But I really don't need the money, and Mother and Father have spoken about using the funds for charity, for things Trip cared about, including perhaps a scholarship at Harvard."

Marcus made a mental note to check that with the parents.

"The funds I was receiving from the trust before Trip died amounted to close to two million a year. That's more than enough to live on, even in Boston."

Marcus laughed.

"And, as I told the police, the day Trip died, I was in Kennebunkport. We had our annual Fourth of July open house, with people dropping by, anytime from noon to midnight. So scores of witnesses can vouch for me, including the vice-president, who stopped by briefly."

"I see," Marcus replied. The vice-president for an alibi. Can't beat that. "Thank you for explaining, and thanks for meeting. I'm sure you're very busy."

David stood and shook Marcus's hand again. He seemed relieved that the meeting was over. "Of course. We want to find out what happened. I don't think Mother will be able to move past this unless we know why Trip died."

Marcus watched David walk back across Beacon Street, a man in a hurry. *Another dead end*, he thought. He walked down Beacon Street and then down Charles to the T station, past restaurants and shops and the place where he'd once bought a leather jacket, in hopes of looking more butch. He wore it once or twice, felt ridiculous, and stowed it in the depths of his closet. *Maybe Bob can wear it*, he found himself thinking.

That evening Marcus wandered around Harvard Square trying to think of next steps. He needed to talk to the parents again, that much was clear. He stopped at a coffee shop and ordered chocolate cake and espresso for dinner, then walked back to Kirkland Street and fell asleep reading Emerson.

"Waldo, you may have been a genius, but your prose style sucks," he murmured to himself as he drifted off.

15

Bob arrived on Wednesday, all smiles. He'd baked a sponge cake and chocolate brownies that he presented to Marcus with a flourish. That day and the next, Marcus worked at the library while Bob began looking for a job. He said he hoped to find something interesting but said would take anything that paid his way through the year he was taking off before starting law school, and maybe allowed him to save a little. His parents were generously supporting him through the summer until he found something.

It seemed to be unspoken that he would move in with Marcus.

In late afternoon when Marcus came home, they would make love. Years later, after it became clear what gay men were dealing with, they reflected on these months, and realized how lucky they were to have found each other. In 1985, solid information about AIDS was in short supply, except for the fact that gay men were at incredible risk. Doctors were telling them not to get tested. "You'd be turning yourself into a pariah for no good reason," Marcus's Harvard doctor told him. "We wouldn't be able to help you."

Marcus thought hard about that word, "pariah." "So what do I do?" he had asked his doctor.

"Stay monogamous with someone you trust."

And then Marcus found Bob. For the first time in his life he felt truly lucky. Blessed.

After their afternoon sessions Bob would get up and cook, humming a song, often early Beatles. He was a magician in the kitchen, one of those people who could open the refrigerator, see what was there, and create something out of nothing.

On Friday of that first week in Cambridge, Marcus had a ten o'clock appointment with his therapist, Gary Williams, who lived in Brookline, a short walk from one of the branches of the Green line on the Boston T. *Boy, do I have a lot to tell him*, Marcus thought on the train as he gathered himself for the session.

Because Gary had been one of the first openly gay therapists in Boston, Marcus surmised that much of his work was about coming out: helping men recognize that they were gay, or helping them figure out what kind of gay man they wanted to be. The two of them had concentrated on the question of casual sex when the therapy began, and Marcus now felt comfortable with his decision that it wasn't really what he wanted, especially given the raging AIDS crisis. They moved on to issues Marcus thought of as deeper—his work, his job, his place in the world. That was where they had run into trouble; Gary didn't seem to have much patience with those issues.

"Look," he said one day. "You're at Harvard. That's the pinnacle. You can do anything you want."

Marcus didn't feel like he could do anything he wanted; he felt confined to a narrow and strict set of professional rules about what he should be doing—writing all the time, publishing constantly. Those rules felt more and more like a pair of shoes that were too tight. Yes, you could walk in them, but why would you want to? And if he didn't wear the shoes, then what?

Marcus arrived a few minutes early and rang the bell. Gary saw clients at his home, the first floor of a renovated duplex. Clients were to ring the bell, then walk into a waiting room, which at one point had been a front hall of some sort. On one side were French doors to the living room, and on the other a door that led to what must have been a bedroom but was now the office. Marcus was surprised that the French doors offered an open view of the living room, which gave hints of the kind of person who lived here: neat, stylish, well off.

Gary opened the office door and Marcus entered. Gary settled into his orthopedic chair, picked up his pen, and, as usual, waited for Marcus to speak. Marcus sat on the couch.

"I'm investigating a murder. And I'm having a relationship with one of the suspects."

For the first time, Marcus saw a look of surprise on Gary's face. No, not surprise. Shock. Marcus let his words sink in and enjoyed the moment. Then he told the story, emphasizing that Bob wasn't really a suspect, at least not in his eyes.

When he got to the end, Gary asked, "So, what are your feelings for this young man?"

"I really like him. I enjoy being with him. There's something about him—something centered. Confident, in a quiet sort of way. He's funny. Charming."

"And all that appeals to you?"

"It does. At least it does with him."

"And the physical relationship?"

Marcus sighed. "Wonderful. Amazing."

Gary smiled widely, another first. "Well, all right."

They talked about something that worried Marcus—the ten-year age difference. Gary said it would only be an issue if Marcus let it become one, that he knew lots of happy couples with as much difference in their ages or more. And he mentioned a study that found that gay male couples with an age difference tended to be happier, stay together longer.

Toward the end of the fifty minutes Marcus said he'd probably be going back and forth to Miller's Cove, so perhaps they shouldn't try to meet again until September. Gary agreed; he'd already told Marcus he took several weeks off in August.

Marcus rode the T to Park Street then transferred to the Red Line for Cambridge. That was the maddening thing about the Boston T; its tracks were like spokes on a wheel, centering around the Boston Common. If you wanted to get from one spoke to the other, you had to go back to the hub.

But today Marcus didn't mind because he had arranged to meet Bob in Harvard Square for an early lunch. Then they packed up and drove back to Miller's Cove in Bob's car, which, in typical Cambridge fashion, had gotten two parking tickets.

"So, where are we with the case, Sherlock?"

"I don't know. Nowhere. The police say a murderer needs motive, means, and opportunity. There's just no one who really has a motive, much less the other two. Unless I'm overlooking something. Or unless there's something I haven't found yet."

Bob thought for a minute. "I wonder if the police have had any better luck."

"Maybe. I'll give that lieutenant a call when we get in."

When they got to town they went grocery shopping and

then back to Bob's place. While Bob put away the groceries Marcus dialed the police station. Fitzgerald picked up on the first ring.

"Lieutenant, Marcus George here. I wonder if you've had any breaks in the case."

"I'm afraid not. So far every possible suspect has an alibi. It was the Fourth of July; everybody was at a party or a picnic or something, surrounded by witnesses."

"I see."

"We'll keep plugging away, but I'm not too hopeful, to be honest. Sorry I don't have better news."

"Lieutenant, I paid a sympathy call on the family in Kennebunkport, and they are clearly extremely well off. I wonder if you've looked at money as a possible motive. Conceivably even someone within the family who would benefit from Trip's death?"

"We thought of that right off the bat. The person who benefits is the elder brother, but he has an airtight alibi, and besides, he's so well off in his own right that it just makes no sense. He has a very generous income from the same family trust fund, and on top of that, he made good money on his own as a corporate attorney before running for office. And, cherry on top, he's about to marry a very rich girl."

So David was not a real suspect. It was a farfetched theory in any case. Marcus thanked the lieutenant and reported the conversation to Bob.

"So what now?" Bob asked.

"I need to talk to the parents again."

"Not today, we need to do laundry."

"Killjoy."

They drove to the local laundromat. Marcus read a biography of Emerson while Bob started a letter to his parents in Connecticut.

"A letter? You're writing an actual letter?" Marcus was surprised; no one these days was writing letters.

"Mom says she likes my penmanship."

"Tell me about your family."

"Not much to tell. June and Ward Cleaver meet Ozzie and Harriet, Ricky and David. Except little Ricky turned out to be queer."

"And they're okay with that?"

"Amazingly, yes. They said they knew all along and wondered when I'd get around to telling them. I had a boyfriend for a while at Brown, and my parents were always inviting him to stay, and not in the guest room either."

"Wow."

"And yours?" Bob asked.

Marcus thought about how best to put it. "Polite disappointment, nothing ever really said out loud, but clear. At least to me."

"I'm sorry," Bob said simply.

"So what happened to the boyfriend?" Marcus asked.

"He dropped me for a woman. They married when we all graduated."

"Ouch."

Bob shrugged.

"And how do you know about the Cleavers and the Nelsons? Those shows are from the fifties."

"'Television and American Culture.' A course at Brown. I got an A."

"Huh."

"You no doubt watched the original broadcasts?" Bob teased.

"You are skating on very thin ice, my boy, if you ever

want to see me naked again." Bob smirked.

When they got home, Bob pulled off Marcus's shirt. "Not bad for an old man," he said, running his hand down Marcus's back, kissing his neck.

16

Later, Marcus called Kennebunkport. The butler answered and Mr. Howard came on the line quickly. Marcus said he wanted to report in and arranged to visit the next day.

"Why don't you come for lunch. Around twelve-thirty?"

Bob got up early the next morning and went to the local gym; Marcus read for a few hours. Marcus thought that Bob was a bit obsessive about the gym, but he knew that was becoming the norm among gay men. The AIDS crisis was pushing people to want to develop more muscle, look stronger and healthier.

Marcus dressed carefully—long slacks, his best polo shirt—and made the short drive to Kennebunkport. The butler let him in.

Mrs. Howard was just descending the stairs, looking somewhat better than the last time Marcus had seen her. She was wearing a silk blouse and matching slacks in yellow. She took Marcus's hand.

"It's good of you to come. We're out on the terrace." Her husband was already there, drinking what looked like a Bloody Mary.

"Would you like one?"

"Thanks, no, I'm driving."

An elegant glass table had been set for three. The flagstone terrace was surrounded by tall trees that provided just enough shade, and Marcus could feel the breeze coming off the ocean. The table was set impeccably: flowers in the middle, old china, heavy silverware that had probably been in the family for two hundred years.

Mrs. Howard pointed to a chair. "Please."

They sat, and the butler began serving lunch. There was gazpacho and what tasted like homemade bread, then lobster over salad with a delicate dressing.

"What a lovely setting," Marcus said.

"Yes, thanks," Mrs. Howard said. "This place has been in the family for nearly a century. We love it here. The boys did too." They made small talk for a while, about Miller's Cove, about Harvard.

"So," Mr. Howard finally said. "What can you tell us?" Both parents put down their forks.

"I'm afraid not much. I've looked into a few things, but so far nothing that suggests who might have committed the crime." A look of disappointment settled on both their faces.

"I'm sorry, I wish I had more. And I know the police aren't getting anywhere either."

"No, they're not," Mr. Howard said. "As we suspected."

"I do have some questions, though."

"Please." Mr. Howard resumed eating.

"I spoke to David, and my understanding is that the income that was going to Trip now goes to him. Is that correct? I hope you don't mind my asking."

"No, not at all. It's a natural question. You are correct about the terms of the trust. It was established long ago, and legally it's airtight. We couldn't change things even if we wanted to, which we don't."

. "And David said you're thinking of using Trip's funds for charity?"

"We are considering that, yes," Mrs. Howard said. "Things that he cared about. The environment. Access to places like Harvard for those without means. We'd like to establish a scholarship in his name."

"I think that would be wonderful," Marcus said, and she smiled.

"I wonder: Did Trip have a room here? Did the police search it?"

"They did," Mr. Howard said. "They didn't find anything out of the ordinary."

"What about his room in your home on Beacon Hill?"

Mr. Howard looked a bit surprised. "No, as far as we know, no one has checked there. It's rather empty."

"Would you mind if I take a look? Just in case something might offer a lead of some kind."

"Of course," Mrs. Howard said. "Any time you like. Mrs. Sanders, the housekeeper, can let you in."

Dessert was crème brûlée and more of their amazing coffee. They lingered a bit, all of them enjoying the breeze rustling gently through the trees. Finally Mrs. Howard got up and said, "Please excuse me, I'm meeting a friend." She shook Marcus's hand and smiled again.

As they went back into the house, Mr. Howard asked Marcus if he would speak at Trip's memorial service, which would take place in ten days or so.

"Yes, of course. I'd be honored."

"It will be a very simple affair, at Memorial Church. It's summer, and most of Trip's friends have graduated and left, of course, so we don't think there will be a huge crowd. But if you could say a few words, we'd be grateful."

Again the gratitude of the rich, Marcus thought as he drove back to Miller's Cove.

At Bob's house he found a note in the kitchen. "At the beach. Meet me at Veranda at five. I'll be the one with a red carnation in my lapel."

Marcus grinned and grabbed his Emerson. He was sound asleep within ten minutes. He woke around four, took a shower, and set off for the Veranda. As he walked along he passed French Canadian couples, some with children, and gay men returning from the beach, some alone, some in groups of two or three. Everyone looked happy, carefree.

It was early and the Veranda wasn't too crowded. Bob had snagged a table in a far corner. Marcus joined him.

"Where's the carnation?"

Bob smirked. Marcus was coming to love that smirk. "And what was your name again?"

"Very funny," Bob said. They ordered drinks, and Marcus told him about lunch.

"Do you really think the brother might have killed Trip for money?"

"No, I don't, and neither do the police. For one thing, the family is loaded. The fortune originated on the father's side in railroads, on the mother's side in cotton, and slavery, of course." Marcus had done some digging, and had contacted an economist at Yale who wrote about large American family fortunes.

"The grandparents were worth close to a billion dollars each, at a time when there weren't all that many billionaires. They set up the trusts."

"The rich really are different," Bob said.

"You're telling me."

"Go on."

"And David has an alibi for the day Trip died. And he must have known the police would look into the finances and that would cast suspicion on him. To top it off, he's about to marry an heiress. No, it just doesn't add up."

Bob agreed. "Let's go back to the house. I need a shower."

Marcus put a hand to his forehead. "You just want to attack my virtue."

"Honey, you don't have any left."

For dinner they made a large salade niçoise, then strolled down to the bakery in town and bought coffee and dessert: cherry tart for Marcus, brownie for Bob. It was another beautiful summer night and they lingered around town.

Bob assumed his Watson role. "So what next, Mr. Holmes?"

"Trip's room on Beacon Hill. Apparently the police haven't searched it. Maybe there's something there."

"When?"

"Monday. We'll go back to town. You need to find a job to support me in the style to which I plan to become accustomed."

Another smirk. "Fat chance, old man."

17

On Sunday afternoon, Marcus called Kennebunkport to say he'd like to look through Trip's room on Beacon Hill the next day. David answered the phone, said he'd make the arrangement with the housekeeper, and gave Marcus the phone number there.

"I'm going to cook you dinner tonight," Marcus said that evening.

"Eek," was all Bob said.

Marcus walked down to the grocery store and bought a cut-up chicken fryer and asparagus. He stopped at the bakery for a cheesecake. Back at the house he prepared the chicken the only way he knew how, doused in Soy Sauce. Bob looked skeptical but said nothing while Marcus made the salad and steamed the asparagus.

"You know, this isn't half bad," Bob said about the chicken. The asparagus was done to just the right degree, nice and crispy, and they ate the salad after the main meal, chatting about this and that, on and off. Marcus loved the fact that their silences were comfortable. *That must mean something,* he thought. They went out to sit on the front porch before attacking the cheesecake.

"Do you think we'll ever find out what happened to

Trip?" Bob asked.

"I don't know. None of it adds up. None of the leads go anywhere. Can you think of anything else about the days leading up to the Fourth?"

Bob was silent for a while. By now Marcus could tell when he was thinking; his brow crinkled a bit.

"No. I've been over it in my head a hundred times. The thing is, we really led separate lives. We were just sharing a house for a summer. We hardly saw each other, didn't talk much. I wish we'd talked more, it might have helped."

"There's no way you could have known what would happen."

"No. Clearly."

Marcus went inside, sliced the cheesecake, and made coffee. He put the things on a tray and carried them out to the porch.

"Cheesecake. Our heritage is showing. But God, is it delicious," Bob said.

"Now, what do I get as my reward for making dinner?"

"Why, Captain Butler, how you talk."

Back in Cambridge on Monday, Marcus arranged to meet the housekeeper at Louisburg Square at 2:30. He took the T and walked the short distance to the Howard townhouse. One of the great things about Louisburg Square, he realized, was how close it was to Charles Street, but at the same time far enough away to feel like a different world, quiet and serene. The streets on this part of Beacon Hill were cobblestone, and Marcus could easily imagine the sound of horse's hooves and Irish policemen saying "Top o' the morning" to the local residents. The townhouses were red brick, the trees and the flowers surrounding them immaculate.

Almost all the original buildings had been preserved, restored. He found #14 on the Square, climbed the steps, rang the bell at the imposing front door. After a moment a thin sixty-ish woman dressed in a simple gray dress opened the door.

"Professor George."

She showed Marcus in, and he caught a glimpse of the front parlor, beautifully and simply furnished, with a bowfront window looking out on the Square, a fireplace, and what looked like a Kandinsky over the mantel. The floors were polished wood, and there was a large Oriental rug, delicately woven.

"This way, please. The room is on the fourth floor."

Marcus thought the housekeeper could have played Mrs. Danvers in *Rebecca*. She directed Marcus to a wood-paneled elevator, discreetly placed off a hallway, and rode up with him. On the fourth floor landing Marcus saw that there were three bedrooms, one very large facing the Square, and two somewhat smaller rooms at the back of the house, facing Charles Street and the river. The housekeeper pointed to one of the two smaller rooms and said she would be in the kitchen on the lower level if he needed anything. The other small bedroom, she said, was "Master David's."

Trip's room was decorated in a tasteful green. There were twin beds, a chest of drawers, and a desk against the window. A door led to a bathroom shared with David's room. Bookshelves on one wall contained the sort of books Trip would have read growing up, novels from high school, history texts, a chemistry textbook.

Marcus opened the closet. A few shirts, a pair of jeans, and, incongruously, an expensive-looking tuxedo. He walked over to the desk. The top was clear except for a blotter and a

simple lamp. The view was out to the back of the buildings
that lined West Cedar, the next street over; Marcus looked
down and saw several lovely gardens. He sat on the desk chair
and opened all the drawers. Writing paper, pens, a pamphlet
from the local Democratic party.

Marcus frowned. Nothing. He went over to the dresser.
Two drawers were empty, two were half full of old clothes,
underwear, athletic socks, sweaters, sweat pants. Marcus
rifled through them and found nothing more. He did catch a
whiff of the cologne Trip wore, Grey Flannel.

He went into the bathroom and once again found
nothing out of the ordinary. David's bedroom on that side
of the house was completely empty. The large room across
the hall was probably a guest room, with a big canopy bed
and a desk that looked like original Queen Anne. More dead
ends.

He went back to Trip's room for a moment and stood
there thinking. As he turned to leave, the sun came shining
through the window, and he paused. He turned around for
another look out the window, and his eyes settled on the
desk. He went over to the blotter and lifted it up.

Underneath were two slips of scratch paper, both with
phone numbers. One was a 917 area code, New York City,
the other 508, central Massachusetts and the Cape. Marcus
scribbled the numbers in his notepad, then took the elevator
down to the kitchen and thanked the housekeeper. She
walked him to the door.

When he got back to his apartment, Bob was baking
brownies. At this rate, Marcus was going to gain ten pounds
and Bob would leave him.

"How did the job hunt go?"

Bob had had an interview that morning with a local attorney.

"Not bad. It could be interesting work. Somewhat. We'll see."

Marcus kissed him on the back of his neck. Bob turned around and kissed him on the lips.

"You only love me for my cooking."

"Well, yeah, and your body. What did you think?"

Bob slapped his butt.

"Oh! You didn't tell me you were into that. That's a different story."

Bob smirked and went back to baking. Marcus sat down at his desk and dialed the first number, the one in New York.

A male voice answered. "Fire Island Productions." Marcus quickly hung up.

He was familiar with the name. It was a company that made very raunchy gay porn.

18

Marcus didn't know what to think. Had Trip known someone who worked there? Was it conceivable he had worked for them, or made porn? It was hard to imagine. Given his background, the life waiting for him, that would have been incredibly dangerous. Marcus told Bob what had just happened.

"Maybe Trip didn't want the life his family expected. Anyway, it seems to me you have two choices. One, we can watch all their porn."

Marcus smiled.

"Two, you can go to New York and talk to them, see if they knew Trip."

"Yes, you're right." Marcus paused. "And even if Trip isn't actually in any of the porn, we still wouldn't know what he was up to, exactly. I need to speak to them."

"True."

"So I guess I'm going to New York."

"We could drive down to Connecticut, stop at my house on the way, or the way back."

Marcus understood: Bob was inviting him to meet his parents. He gulped. "Really? Are you sure you want to do that now?"

Bob came over and put his arms around him. "You have got to taste my mother's cooking. Cold borscht to die for."

"Oh, well, for borscht . . ." Marcus said. "Let's do it."

They left early the next morning. It was about three hours to Danbury, and Bob called ahead and said they'd be there for lunch. Marcus drove, Bob gave him directions.

The house was on a beautiful tree-lined street, green lawns and old oaks. Children were playing in the front yards, running through sprinklers.

"I see what you mean. Ozzie and Harriet definitely could have lived here."

"Not to mention the Cleavers."

The house was a large center-hall colonial, that beloved New England style. The lawn was well tended and flowers grew all around the house. Everything was perfect. Marcus suddenly felt nervous.

Bob let himself in with a key just as his mother came out with a huge smile and hugged him. "Welcome, Marcus," she said, and then, to his surprise, hugged him too. She was a lovely woman in her late forties, a Jewish version of Mrs. Howard, but much more simply dressed, shorts and a striped blouse. She was trim and athletic. Bob had said she played a lot of tennis.

"Did you make borscht, as requested, hmm?" Bob teased.

"Yes, and it's all ready." She laughed. Marcus could see that parts of Bob looked like her; he had her nose and chin.

They both washed their hands in the powder room. Marcus caught sight of a big living room, a dining room, a den, and a room that looked like a study, piled with books and papers. Not Kennebunkport, to be sure, but a comfortable, upper-middle-class home. The family that lived here had made it safely to the suburbs.

Mrs. Abramson led them to a breakfast room flooded with sun, overlooking the back yard, with French doors leading to a shady patio. It was a hot day, so the doors were closed and they ate inside, tucked into the central air conditioning. Bob's mother explained that her husband was at work and was sorry to miss Marcus, but would see him later.

Bob was right, the borscht was to die for. It was served with plain yogurt, and Marcus had never tasted anything like it. There was also home-baked bread—Marcus saw where Bob got that knack—and salad and iced tea and homemade chocolate chip cookies. They talked and talked. Mrs. Abramson asked Marcus what he taught, what he was working on, and Bob asked her about various neighbors and old friends. Within fifteen minutes, Marcus realized he felt comfortable.

After one last cookie, Marcus stood. "Thank you for lunch, Mrs. Abramson, it was wonderful. I hate to leave, but I don't want to miss my train."

"Please, call me Ruth. And be careful in the big bad city." She laughed again.

Bob drove him the short distance to the station in the family Volvo wagon. "So?" he asked.

"So, what?" Marcus pretended puzzlement.

"What did you think?"

"You were right, the borscht was amazing."

Bob gave him a look.

"She's lovely. The house is lovely. The neighborhood is lovely. I'm beginning to wonder if this is Stepford village, the Jewish version."

Bob laughed, his mother's laugh. "Call me when you know what train you'll be taking back. And be careful."

19

Marcus got to Grand Central Terminal in Manhattan in just over an hour. A blast of heat and noise assaulted him as he left the station. He hailed a taxi and gave the driver the address he had been given when he called that morning and said he needed to speak to the manager or owner, letting them know what time he expected to get there. He told the person answering the phone that he was investigating the death of someone who might have had contact with their company, being purposely vague about what kind of investigation and what kind of death.

An expensive, hair-raising cab ride later, he was dripping with sweat and standing in front of a warehouse in the nether reaches of Brooklyn. There was a steel door with a doorbell. When a voice came over the intercom, Marcus gave his name and said he was expected. He was buzzed in.

He found himself in a stark waiting room with a lumpy couch and not much else. A young gay man came out through another steel door.

"This way."

Marcus followed him past some offices into a huge open space with a very high ceiling. A movie was being filmed. There were lights, cameras, crew members, and a huge mattress on the floor against a wall painted sky blue. Out of camera range was a shelf holding various sex toys, leather equipment, and cameras.

Lounging on the mattress was a young man dressed in nothing but a leather harness. He had covered himself with a towel. Standing just off to the side were two slightly older musclemen, wearing leather harnesses and leather boots. Both had put on bathrobes. All three of them were sweating despite the air conditioning; they had clearly been filming. They and the crew members looked Marcus over head to toe.

The director, a man of about fifty, turned around and introduced himself as Michael Stone. Marcus loved porn names, they were all so obvious, and ridiculous.

"I'm Marcus George. Is there somewhere we could talk?"

"Sorry, no, we're behind schedule. What do you need?"

Marcus pulled out Trip's picture. The director and the two musclemen stared at it. One of them smirked. "He was great in the sack."

Marcus suppressed his shock as Stone turned to the cast and the crew. "This young man is dead," Marcus said.

Everyone looked stunned.

"Take ten," Stone said, and showed Marcus to one of the offices he'd passed on his way in.

It was a simple office with a steel desk, a few chairs, and a transom window. Stone closed the door and leaned against the desk. He lit a cigarette.

"Did you know this young man?" Marcus asked.

"Who are you again?"

"My name is Marcus George. The family has asked me to look into this young man's death. I discovered your phone number among his things."

Stone sat down.

"Okay," he said, then paused. Marcus wondered whether he was trying to remember, or figuring out the best story to tell.

"He contacted me a few months ago, I don't remember exactly when. He said he wanted to shoot porn, maybe be in it, maybe direct, and that he could finance some films. He came down to New York one weekend, and I needed to find out if he had the right stuff, so I arranged for him to spend the night with Brock." Brock was presumably the first muscleman.

"And?"

"Brock said he was great. The kid had the looks, and Brock said he had the body. The kid said he'd be available to film in the fall, that he was graduating from college and would be moving to New York at the end of the summer."

"He graduated from Harvard."

Stone looked taken aback. "No shit," he muttered.

"Did you hear from him again?" Marcus asked.

"No. I figured he'd call when he was ready. We get a lot of calls like that, guys who want to do porn, or think they do. Some of them chicken out, some follow through. Happens all the time."

"Was it unusual that he offered to finance some films?"

"Yeah, that was unusual. Very. But he looked like money—the way he dressed, his style. The car he drove."

Marcus thought for a moment, letting it all sink in.

"How did he die?" Stone asked.

"He was murdered. Up in Maine." Marcus let that sink in. Stone turned pale.

"Any idea what might have happened to him?" Marcus asked.

"Jesus, no. I just talked to him that one weekend. And

hey, somebody with a hot bod offers me money to be in my movies, I'm not gonna knock him off. We're always looking for financing. All this is expensive." He gestured out to the warehouse space.

Marcus had to admit that made sense. He asked if he could speak to Brock. Stone called him into the office, and Marcus repeated what he had told Stone, that Trip had been murdered. Brock, if that was really his name, looked genuinely upset.

"Did anything strange or unusual happen when you were together?" Marcus asked.

"No." Brock hesitated a bit. "We met here, then went to my place and talked. I explained what needed to happen— that we needed to get it on, to see if he had the right stuff. It was a Sunday, no one else was here."

"And?"

"He was into it. We got naked and played. He was hot, really hot. He seemed to enjoy himself." Brock paused. "When we were done, he took a shower and left."

Marcus thanked both men and gave them his phone numbers in case they thought of something to add. As he made his way to the waiting room, he could see the two remaining porn stars fondling each other.

The young man who had ushered him in appeared and showed him a phone, and he called a cab. He felt relieved when he hit the street, and he got to Grand Central just in time for the 7:10 to Danbury.

He was worn out. And sick at heart. The heat, the travel, the film shoot, the image of Trip making porn. Too much.

Bob picked him up at the station, and Marcus told him what happened. "Can you see Trip doing that?" he asked.

"Hard to imagine. Upsetting. But we know Trip liked sex.

A lot of sex. Is it so farfetched?"

"I guess not," Marcus conceded, and Bob agreed with the obvious conclusion: Stone wouldn't kill someone who wanted to give him money.

Another dead end.

When they got back to Bob's house, they sat in the car for a few minutes. "I'm a little surprised that all these people are talking to you," Bob said.

"I must have an honest face."

"Seriously."

"I guess hearing about a murder shocks people into talking. On some level they must know that if they don't talk to me, they'll have to deal with the police."

"I suppose so. Let's go inside."

Bob's parents were sitting in the den talking. Mozart played in the background. Bob's father got up and greeted Marcus warmly. He looked like what Marcus imagined Bob would look like in about thirty years. They could almost have passed for brothers, if not for his father's gray hair. Bob had his physical grace.

"You look like you need a drink."

"I do, Mr. Abramson, absolutely," Marcus said.

"It's Jake, and we're drinking spritzers."

"Perfect."

The telephone rang.

"That will be Jerry. Excuse me." Jake was a lawyer, and Jerry was his partner. They were in the middle of some mess, Ruth explained.

"Are you hungry?" she asked Marcus.

"Yes, as a matter of fact I'm starved." Marcus realized that he hadn't had any dinner.

"Come," Ruth said.

She pulled plates of food out of the refrigerator, and
Jake brought Marcus the spritzer when he got off the phone.
Ruth sliced some homemade bread to accompany the pasta
with tuna, lightly sauced, and tomato and basil salad. Marcus
gobbled it all down and started to relax. He hoped he didn't
look like too much of a pig.

While he ate, Ruth served her men poppy seed cake and
decaf. She offered Marcus a slice of cake when he was done,
but he was stuffed.

"I'll pack up the rest, you can take it back with you
tomorrow," she said.

Bob smiled. "Once a Jewish mother, always a Jewish
mother."

Ruth laughed.

It was now after ten. Jake said he'd be leaving very early
in the morning so he probably wouldn't see them again. He
hugged his son and shook Marcus's hand. After washing the
dishes, Marcus and Bob retired to Bob's old room. Marcus
took a shower and slept like the dead.

20

He woke up at 7:45, and Bob wasn't in the other twin bed. Marcus stuck his head out the door and heard him talking and laughing with his mother in the kitchen. He was amazed at how easy they seemed together, how natural. Marcus couldn't remember ever laughing with his mother.

He went into the bathroom, brushed his teeth, washed his face, and put on a terrycloth robe that had materialized out of nowhere. He went down to the kitchen.

Bob was in a T-shirt and shorts, Ruth in another pair of shorts and a simple top. She looked way too cheerful for eight in the morning. They were gabbing away about Bob's older brother and his family in California. Marcus gathered there was a new grandchild in Los Angeles. The French doors to the garden were open, and it was blessedly cool. Ruth was making a huge omelet, which they ate out on the patio with strong coffee and sourdough toast. Marcus began to feel like a human being again.

"Why don't you stay a few days," Ruth said. "The Baskin-Robbins has a new flavor of the month." They all chuckled. Bob glanced at Marcus and said no, they needed to get back. Ruth smiled and said she understood.

In the front hall as they were leaving, Ruth handed Bob

a package—the remains of the poppy-seed cake and a large batch of chocolate chip cookies. Marcus wondered why they all didn't weigh two hundred pounds.

"Come back soon," Ruth said. Marcus thanked her for everything, and they were off.

When they got back to Cambridge, they went straight to the soup and salad place for lunch. Then Bob went back to Kirkland Street and Marcus stopped at his office. After going through the mail, he took out the second phone number he had found in Trip's Beacon Hill room. He dialed it.

"Congressman Denby's office."

Marcus hung up. Denby was an extremely conservative Republican member of Congress from central Massachusetts.

Trip was full of surprises.

Marcus considered the possibilities. Trip had called the congressman to complain about one of his votes. Or to apply for a job; Marcus knew other liberal students who went to work for conservative politicians or organizations, wanting to know the enemy.

Or something else.

How to find out?

He walked back to Kirkland Street and found a note from Bob, who was grocery shopping. He called the congressman's number again and explained that he'd like to come in to talk about an important matter; when would the congressman be available? The secretary who answered the phone asked him to hold on.

After a long wait, a male voice came on the line. "This is Ron Adams, I'm Congressman Denby's aide. May I ask what this is in reference to?"

Marcus decided to tell the exact truth: he was looking into the death of a young Harvard graduate at the request of the family, he found this number, wondered if the congressman or anyone in his office could shed any light. There was a long pause.

"I suggest you put your request in a letter and send it here." He gave Marcus an address in Springfield, in the center of the State. "Good afternoon."

The brush-off.

Marcus considered his options. He could write the letter. He could just show up in Springfield, or even in the congressman's Washington office. Or he could turn the information over to Lieutenant Fitzgerald.

He decided official channels were best. A congressman was no one to fool around with. Nor was a police lieutenant.

He dialed Fitzgerald's number. The lieutenant picked up on the second ring, and Marcus told him about finding the phone number and about the conversation he had just had.

Fitzgerald was clearly intrigued. He said to give him a day or so to figure out what to do and that he'd let Marcus know.

Marcus and Bob spent the next two days falling into what they later thought of as their summer routine. They slept late. In the afternoon they usually made love. Bob cooked, Marcus did the dishes. Marcus spent a few hours every day at the library or his office, and Bob had job interviews.

Marcus could hardly remember feeling so content.

On the morning of the third day, a Thursday, the phone rang while they were still in bed, and Marcus pulled himself up to answer it. It was Fitzgerald.

"You and I are meeting the congressman in his office today at three. Give me your address; I'll pick you up at twelve thirty."

When he put down the phone, Marcus groaned and collapsed back on the bed.

"What the hell am I doing?" he asked out loud.

Finally he got himself up, dressed, ate toast, drank coffee, and at 12:30 went downstairs to wait.

Fitzgerald arrived on time in his unmarked police car. There was heavy traffic as usual getting out of Boston but then smooth driving. They made small talk along the way. Marcus learned that Fitzgerald grew up in Worcester, which they passed on the Mass Pike, and that his father, uncle, and grandfather had been or were police officers there.

They arrived at in a nondescript office building in downtown Springfield just after three and took the elevator to the fourth floor, as instructed. They were kept waiting for twenty minutes, and Fitzgerald was getting agitated, tapping his foot. Finally they were ushered into an inner office.

The congressman rose and shook their hands. He was around fifty, tall, dressed in the standard Washington-issue blue Brooks Brothers suit.

"So tell me about this unfortunate young man."

Marcus showed him the photo, and Fitzgerald filled in a few details. They both watched him carefully as he studied the photo.

"Look," the congressman said after a very long pause. Marcus could see the wheels turning in his head.

"I know this is a serious investigation, so I'm going to tell you the truth. We met by accident at Logan." Logan was Boston's airport. "It was last February, and there was a blizzard. Everything was grounded." Marcus remembered that Trip had said in February that he was going to D.C. to look at some manuscripts at the Library of Congress that might be relevant to his thesis.

"We started talking and then had a bite to eat. The snow was still coming down, so I called my office and had them arrange a room at the airport hotel."

There was another pause.

"I invited Mr. Howard to join me for the night. In the morning the planes were flying, and we went our separate ways. I never saw him again."

"Did you give him your office phone number?"

"No, I did not. Though it's easy enough to find."

Fitzgerald asked the obvious question. "Did you have sexual relations?"

The congressman looked down and closed his eyes for a moment. "Yes."

The word hung in the air.

"And you never heard from him or saw him again?"

"No. Never. I spent a very pleasant night with him, and that was that."

Marcus couldn't help himself. "So you're gay?"

The Congressman tried hard to control himself. "That, Professor, is none of your business."

Fitzgerald shot Marcus a disapproving look and asked Denby his whereabouts on the Fourth of July.

"In the morning I was at home with my family, and then I attended a picnic here in Springfield with about two hundred other people. I was there from three until ten."

Fitzgerald thanked him for answering their questions and motioned to Marcus that it was time to leave.

In the car, they both looked at each other.

"So what was that?" Marcus asked.

Fitzgerald was clearly uncomfortable. "It was a married Republican congressman admitting that he had, um, 'gay,' um, sex, once, with an attractive young man he happened to run into."

"Could that have led to murder?"

"On what motive?"

"Well, it wouldn't be blackmail, Trip had plenty of money. But maybe Trip wanted to expose him as a hypocrite. Lots of gay men have that instinct."

"Maybe," Fitzgerald responded. "But would he have told the congressman he was going to expose him? Not very likely. Why the phone number, why not just call a reporter?"

Marcus pondered.

"And besides, what proof would Trip have had?" Fitzgerald seemed to be thinking out loud. "It would have been he said, he said."

"Well, there would have been the hotel record."

"Yes, but the congressman's staff booked the room. Nothing unusual there. Unless they ordered from room service and someone else saw them being cozy, really cozy, and could remember and would testify to that. It was several months ago. And even if there was a witness, a witness to what? Two guys stranded in a hotel."

"Too farfetched?" Marcus asked.

"Kinda. Dunno. Have to think about it."

On the way back to Boston they hit rush hour, neither saying very much. Finally they arrived at Marcus's building. Before he got out of the car, Fitzgerald spoke.

"I don't think so. I can't see that guy killing Trip, somehow escaping a well-attended event to drive to Miller's Cove, shoot someone, and drive all the way back to Springfield. It's got to be at least three or four hours each way, more on a holiday. That's at least six hours of driving plus the murder. We'll check out his story, but if he was in Springfield all day, he couldn't have done it."

"I guess you're right."

"The trail has gone cold, I'm afraid."

Fitzgerald looked worn out, and still had to drive back to Maine. Marcus realized Fitzgerald reminded him of John Wayne playing Sean Thornton in *The Quiet Man*, minus perhaps twenty pounds. He wore a wedding ring, and Marcus assumed he was going home to a wife who looked just like Maureen O'Hara. He was astounded to learn much later that the lieutenant was married to a Jewish woman from Brooklyn who sounded like Barbra Streisand.

Marcus realized he was starting to think of people in movie terms, as Bob did. He smiled, dragged himself upstairs, and found Bob humming "Oklahoma." The smell of something with tomato sauce filled the apartment. Marcus felt immediately better.

Bob imitated a Jewish mother. "I slave all day over a hot stove and he doesn't even call."

Marcus took him in his arms. "Put it on low. Dinner can wait."

21

"Porn stars, Republican congressmen, I can't make it out. Who was Trip?"

They were eating burnt lasagna and a salad, mostly naked.

Bob looked up from his plate. "He was a handsome, rich gay boy who could have had anything, and almost anyone. Any life he wanted. And he didn't know who he was."

Marcus realized that Bob, for all his youth, was remarkably perceptive and mature.

"You're right. You're absolutely right. And his family had no idea who he was either."

For dessert they ate the last of Ruth's poppy-seed cake, warmed in the oven.

"We're never gonna know who did it, are we?" Bob asked, sounding sad.

"Doesn't look like it."

Bob reached across the small table and put his hand on top of Marcus's.

"And I don't know how in the hell I'm going to speak at that memorial service next week."

They decided to go back to Miller's Cove for the few days before the service. The weather was a bit hot, and the town and beach were crowded, but they enjoyed themselves, and Marcus felt himself falling more and more in love. He would stare at Bob sleeping and wonder what he had done to deserve someone so wonderful, so funny and smart and sexy. And such a good cook!

In the mornings Bob would go to the gym and Marcus would work, usually at the big desk in the room that had been Trip's. He moved the newspaper clippings and Trip's other things onto the bed so he could spread out. He spent some time on Emerson and struggled with his remarks for the service.

They'd usually go to Maineium's for lunch and then walk down to the gay section of the beach. Marcus still couldn't bring himself to sit under the awning, even though he craved the shade. On the sand in his rented beach chair he would read or doze while Bob swam. They'd pour suntan lotion all over each other and laugh. Marcus burned nevertheless; Bob turned golden brown. For dinner they went out or Bob cooked. They always ended the day sitting out on the porch, listening to the evening sounds.

On Tuesday they drove back to Cambridge for the memorial service, which was scheduled for three p.m. the next day. The apartment was hot, so they took showers and then went to a movie: *Jagged Edge*, Glenn Close defending Jeff Bridges, who was accused of the grisly murder of his rich wife.

Not a good choice.

Back home, Bob went to sleep and Marcus sat up late, obsessing about what to say at the service.

In the morning Marcus was restless, nervous, and didn't want any breakfast. Bob knew to just let him be. When it was time, Marcus put on his best suit and made his way to campus.

Memorial Church was a simple structure, elegant, stately, standing in Harvard Yard across from Widener Library. On nice days students would sit on the steps facing the Yard, eating bag lunches, talking, sometimes drinking wine out of paper bags.

Marcus had been told to come at two o'clock to go through the service with Peter Gomes, Harvard's Protestant chaplain, who was already there. As the chaplain, he would speak first, Gomes explained, then David would speak, then the choir would sing a hymn, then Marcus. The chaplain walked him through where to stand and how to use the microphone. At half-past two the small choir showed up and took their places, and by quarter of three the church was starting to fill up.

Marcus stood to the side, uncomfortably warm in his jacket and tie.

He was amazed at how many people filed into the church. Young people who must have been friends of Trip's; older, prosperous-looking couples and singles who clearly knew the senior Howards. Bob came in, followed by Deena Echols and a man who must have been her husband, along with several other faculty members. Bob caught Marcus's eye and smiled.

As Marcus smiled back, he was flabbergasted to see the governor walk in with the university president, then Trip's parents and David, with a stunning young woman who must have been his fiancée. The Howards sat in the front row, Governor Dukakis and President Bok just behind them. Marcus sat at the opposite end of the front row with the chaplain.

So much for a small service, Marcus thought to himself. He tried to calm his nerves. He hadn't expected to be speaking in front of the university president and the governor. *Thank God no Bushes.*

The Chaplain rose and spoke, but Marcus took in very little of what he said; he was concentrating on the notes in front of him. Then David rose and Marcus listened. David told several anecdotes from their childhood, some funny, some touching, and Marcus could hear people behind him crying. Apparently Trip was quite a trickster, always causing mischief for his older brother, short-sheeting his bed, reaching in and turning off the hot water when David was taking a shower in the bathroom they shared. David's manner seemed cool to Marcus but then, he reminded himself, Protestants and rich people were different. Showing emotion in public was a faux pas.

David sat and the choir sang the hymn "I Watch the Sunrise." They sang beautifully. Then the chaplain signaled to Marcus, and he rose and walked up to the lectern.

"Trip Howard was the kind of student faculty members dream about," he began. He praised Trip's intellectual excitement and his instinct for grasping the emotional undercurrents behind an academic subject. He went on to describe Trip's passion for justice and to wonder what Trip might have accomplished had he lived, "not only for himself, but for all of us." He ended by reading A. E. Housman's "To an Athlete Dying Young," choking back tears when he came to the line "Smart lad, to slip betimes away."

As he finished he looked over at Trip's parents, who also had tears in their eyes. Marcus took his seat.

The chaplain thanked everyone for coming and invited them to a reception at University Hall. As they all rose, Mrs. Howard came over to Marcus, gave him a hug, then shook hands with the chaplain and went back to her family.

Marcus found Bob. On the way out they ran into Deena Echols. She introduced her husband, Jordan, and Marcus introduced Bob, and they began walking toward University Hall.

"Your little speech was very nice, and I loved the poem," Deena said. "Have you seen *Out of Africa?*"

"Pardon me?" Marcus said.

"It's a new movie with Meryl Streep playing Karen Blixen, who later took the pen name Isak Dinesen, as I'm sure you know."

Marcus didn't know, and Deena went on. "Meryl as Karen reads the same poem at the funeral of her lover, Robert Redford. Very moving."

"I'll have to catch that," Marcus said, reminding himself to check with Bob and noticing that Jordan looked uncomfortable, possibly because of the heat or because he didn't know Trip from Adam.

"Trip was an intelligent young man," Deena continued. "He came to see me about his thesis. Lincoln, wasn't it? I didn't particularly agree with his analysis, but he made it passionately. How did the thesis turn out?"

"Quite well. He graduated *magna*."

At the reception several students Marcus knew came over to chat. The women hugged him, the men shook his hand. He asked them what they were doing this summer and got the usual run of things bright Harvard graduates did. Bob brought him a glass of lukewarm punch.

Trip's father came over to thank Marcus for speaking, and Marcus introduced Bob. Just as they were thinking of leaving, Lieutenant Fitzgerald entered, walked over to Marcus and Bob, and shook both their hands.

"Just thought you'd want to know, the congressman's

story checks out completely," he said sotto voce.

"I see."

"Could he have hired someone to do the actual deed?" Bob asked. Marcus had had the same thought.

"That would be very unusual in a situation like this," the lieutenant said, his voice still low. "For one thing, it's dangerous. The killer can always turn around and blackmail you, especially if you're in politics. Or rich. We usually only see that sort of thing when the mob is involved and where loyalty is guaranteed, or in a criminal gang, and there's no evidence of that sort of involvement."

"So, is it going to remain an unsolved crime?" Marcus half-asked, half-concluded.

"The investigation is still open, but so far we're not getting anywhere."

"Am I still a suspect, lieutenant?" Bob asked.

"Oh God, no. We knew right away. Sorry, I should have told you. Your alibi checked out perfectly." Bob had spent the Fourth at the beach and was at the Veranda at the time of the murder. Both were crowded, and many witnesses remembered seeing him both places.

Slightly embarrassed about not letting Bob off the hook, the lieutenant excused himself to pay his respects to the family. The senior Howards were surrounded by people, so Marcus went over to David to say good-bye. David introduced his fiancée, Caroline Peters, who shook his hand. She had an outsized diamond and emerald ring on her left ring finger, and she was wearing a chic Chanel suit. They chatted for a few minutes, and Marcus saw that they both were quite tan. He said something about getting sun in Kennebunkport.

"Actually, we were in the South of France for a few days, visiting an old friend of mine," Caroline said.

That struck Marcus as a bit odd, given all that was going on, but he realized he knew almost nothing about the lives of the rich. As he excused himself and went back to Bob, Mrs. Howard looked in his direction and gave him a half smile. She was in deep pain, there was no doubt about that.

Finally, they were out in the fresh air. They both loosened their ties and took off their jackets. Bob started walking toward the Square, not Kirkland Street. Marcus followed.

"Where are we going?" Marcus asked.

"In the direction of hard liquor."

22

They drank frozen daiquiris and sat quietly at The Harvest, one of Cambridge's more tony and expensive restaurants. A few people Marcus had seen at the service filtered in. One distinguished-looking man came over and complimented Marcus on the poem, shook his hand. He didn't introduce himself, which was typical of the upper class in Boston and the Harvard elect, Marcus had learned. One was simply expected to know the names of the important people.

"Really, it's true," Bob said. "The poem was just right."

Marcus said he hoped so, and his mood lifted a bit. They decided to stay and order food, but Marcus wasn't very hungry. He was surprised by how emotional he felt. Bob sensed his mood.

"Let's go back to Maine tomorrow?" Marcus said.

"You just want to ogle all the bodies on the beach," Bob teased.

"And your point is . . ."

Marcus laughed.

They went to bed early and cuddled.

They left for Miller's Cove in the morning. It was an overcast day and it felt like rain, so they went straight to the grocery store and then home, or what was beginning to feel like home to Marcus. Or a second home. Or something. Marcus just knew he liked it here. He was beginning not to remember what life was like before Bob and Miller's Cove.

Bob made a salad for lunch, then napped while Marcus sat on the front porch with a book on Hawthorne and watched the rain. After a while he joined Bob in the bedroom, and Bob, half asleep, put his head on his shoulder. Marcus kissed his forehead and slept.

By five the rain had stopped and the sun was out, so they dressed and went to the Veranda for a drink. It was a Thursday evening, and the town was already filling up with the weekend crowd, as usual. To Marcus's surprise, two of the students who had been at the memorial service walked in and came over to say hello. One had been in the first class Trip had taken with Marcus, "American Political Rhetoric." His name was Paul Kinsella, and he introduced his friend as Rob Ellis. Just as Marcus was introducing Bob, a table for four opened up, and they grabbed it.

"I liked your poem," Paul said. Marcus thanked him.

"Do you know if the police are getting anywhere?" Rob asked.

"It doesn't seem like it," Marcus said.

"Bob. Wait. Are you the guy who was sharing a house with Trip?" Paul asked.

"That's right."

"Trip mentioned you. He was really happy to have found a place for the summer here. He didn't want to stay down with his parents."

Bob smiled.

"Tell me," Marcus said, "do you know anything about Trip's personal life that might help the police? Anyone hate him? Any feuds?"

Paul looked uncomfortable and glanced at Rob, who looked down. Finally, Paul spoke. "There was one thing."

Marcus and Bob stared at him intently.

"Trip was seeing a shrink at school, and he really hated her. At first he seemed to like her, but then something happened, I don't know what, but apparently she threatened to have him committed. Or at least that's what Trip said."

Marcus was stunned. "Do you know her name?"

"No. But she's on the Health Center staff. Should be easy to find."

The conversation turned to other things, and after a while, Bob and Marcus got up to go. They all shook hands and murmured the usual niceties about staying in touch.

"I know what you're thinking," Bob said on the walk home. "That shrink, whoever she is, might be the killer. But, really?"

"Unlikely, I guess," Marcus said, but he wondered.

"Who knows what really happened," Bob said. "Let's say Trip hated her. That happens all the time in therapy."

Marcus again realized how sharp Bob was and thought what he had just said was probably true. He had been tempted to lose his temper with his own therapist more than a few times.

"But what about the threat of commitment?" Marcus prodded.

"Unusual, I guess. But did it really happen? Trip could have been exaggerating."

"True," Marcus admitted.

"What are you thinking?"

"Dunno. Have to sleep on it."

"And here I thought you were going to sleep on moi."

Bob batted his long eyelashes. Marcus guffawed.

Over breakfast the next morning, Marcus said he knew what to do.

"I think I should pass the story on to the police. They can check it out. There's no way I could do this; a psychologist isn't going to talk to a third party, even if the client is dead. She might be more open with the police, but even there, she'll be governed by privacy laws."

Bob agreed. After a second cup of coffee Marcus called Lieutenant Fitzgerald and repeated the story.

"Interesting. We'll look into it. Thanks." And that was that.

Marcus and Bob spent the next week in what they both remembered later as a blissful state. They had been together long enough to know and adjust to each other's habits and temperaments. Bob knew just when to say something funny to lighten Marcus's mood, which tended toward the brooding. Marcus knew when Bob wanted to do something alone, the gym or the beach, and when he wanted affection, which was nearly always.

Marcus spent some time each day on his work; Bob had some telephone interviews for jobs and did most of the shopping and cooking. They went to the beach. Both of them felt relaxed. A couple.

At the end of a happy week Lieutenant Fitzgerald called back.

"We located and interviewed Trip's therapist at Harvard, Deborah Sand. She told us very little, other than that they were going through a difficult patch in their therapy when he died. She stressed that was to be expected in most cases. She was out of town over the Fourth, and her alibi checks out. She's not a suspect."

It was what Marcus expected to hear. "Is the case closed, lieutenant?"

"It's getting to that point."

At dinner that night both Marcus and Bob were gloomy and didn't say much. Finally, Bob spoke.

"I think we have to let Trip go. You've done what you can. More than enough. And even if you find the murderer, or the police do, it won't bring him back."

"You're right, of course."

"I think it will be easier to let him go after the summer," Bob said. "After leaving this house." It was now the beginning of August, and the lease Bob had signed was up at the end of September.

Marcus looked around the kitchen. "That's probably true too. Although I really like Miller's Cove. When we're both rich and famous we'll have to buy a house here."

23

The next morning, the phone rang while Marcus was reading, and Bob answered.

"This is Brock Majors. Is Marcus there? Um, tell him we met on the porn set."

Bob handed the phone to Marcus, deadpan. "Your porn star is on the phone."

Marcus was startled. "Hello?"

"This is Brock. We met in New York?"

"Yes, yes, hello."

"Look, I didn't say this when you were here because Stone was there and he would have chewed me out. He doesn't like his actors to see each other except on the set. He thought I was just with your boy once, to see if he was okay. He thinks if his actors see each other too much on our own, we won't get hot enough in the movie."

"Okay. And?"

"Your boy was hot. Super-hot. We really clicked, at least in the sack. And so he came down a few weekends after that first time, stayed at my place. Stone didn't know."

"I see."

"It was just sex. Really good sex, but just sex. I mean, he was graduating from Harvard, for Chrissake. I never even finished high school."

"Thanks for letting me know." Marcus's mind was racing. "Did anything happen while he was with you that you think could be related to what happened to him?"

"No. Nothing, really. Your boy just liked sex."

"Anything else?"

"Well, kinda." There was a long pause. "He had this notebook, and the last time I saw him, he forgot it. I've, uh, I've still got it."

Now Marcus's heart was racing. He asked Brock to send the notebook to him by Federal Express and said he would reimburse him. Brock agreed. Marcus gave him the address.

"Just for the record, Brock, I have to ask this. Where were you on July Fourth?"

"Fire Island with a bunch of guys. We stayed at Stone's house. We filmed a scene. You can check with him."

When Marcus got off the phone, Bob was baking. "So, you're leaving me for a porn star. I get it," he said without looking up. Marcus laughed and told him about the conversation.

All Bob could say was, "Wow!"

The notebook arrived late the next morning. They sat down at the kitchen table and went through it together. Trip wrote in it only occasionally, and it was mostly just a catalog of what he was doing, when, and with whom. Some "thesis going well" comments. Dinner with so-and-so. "Mom called." The earliest entry was from the previous October. There were comments about the weather and a boring lecture class Trip was taking on modern art history. He called it "Dots and Spots." Marcus wondered if his family owned any of the paintings covered in the class.

There were a few innocuous remarks about Deborah, the

therapist, including that "she just doesn't understand what it means to have a dick." One day in January, Trip wrote, she "joked" about committing him to a mental hospital where he couldn't continue being promiscuous.

Trip had obviously embellished that story, or had been misunderstood by his friend. There was nothing about hating the therapist. And he was clearly talking to her about his sex life, maybe even trying to bring it under control, Marcus thought. There were lots of explicit details about his sex partners, who were numerous. And Brock had told the truth; Trip described it as the hottest sex he'd ever had.

Trip also briefly mentioned the tryst at the airport with the congressman, saying, "he wasn't half bad for an old guy." So the congressman was telling the truth, at least about that part of the story.

"I need another shower," Bob said after they had read the last page.

Marcus sighed. "Another dead end."

"Yes. And not something we can show the family."

"No, definitely not."

It was clear from the way Trip wrote about his partners that he felt no emotional attachment to any of them, and that he only saw them once, maybe twice, with the exception of Brock, which meant a jealous boyfriend as the killer was not at all likely, unless it was Brock himself. But Brock had an alibi that would be easy to check, so he wouldn't have lied about that, Marcus thought; he made a mental note to call Stone and ask him about the Fourth. And if Brock had killed Trip, why would he have called Marcus? He'd have thrown the notebook away. As Brock said, it was sex, just sex, for both of them.

"We can't show this to the police. They'd write Trip off

as a total whore, if they haven't already done that, and they'd show it to the family, probably, to see if they knew any of the names . . ." Bob's voice trailed off.

Marcus wasn't sure they didn't have an obligation to give the notebook to the police. But Bob talked him out of it, at least for the time being. Both of them, Bob especially, were growing weary and disheartened by the case, the emotional roller-coaster it had brought them, the pall it cast over the summer.

"Look," Bob said. "The police would try to identify all the names so they could question them. That would be traumatic, disrupt their lives. And for what?"

Bob was probably right about that. Marcus recognized a few of the names as Harvard students. Some of them probably weren't out, or not sure what they were or what they wanted. One was a student who was now engaged to a woman; Marcus felt some obligation to protect all of them. He'd think about it for a few days, decide whether he needed to show the notebook to Fitzgerald.

"I'm surprised he had time for any school work at all," Marcus said, and Bob laughed.

24

Marcus woke early and resolved to get more work done; the summer would be over soon, and he'd be occupied with syllabi and lecture notes and all manner of academic business. He spent the next several mornings working in Trip's old room, caffeine-fueled. He was writing now, and he had some sense of what to write.

Most days he and Bob would go to Maineium's for lunch then head for the beach together. Sometimes, if his scholarly juices were really flowing, Marcus would go home after lunch and Bob would go to the beach alone.

Bob always had a report when he got home after a solo trip to the beach.

"I'm leaving you for that guy in the pink bathing suit. He's coming over to help me pack."

"A Hollywood director offered me a part in his next film."

"A stockbroker from New York wants to marry me."

Marcus always laughed.

After a good week when he accomplished quite a bit, Marcus hit a snag in his writing. As he usually did when that happened, he got up and started furiously pacing around Trip's room. It was early on a rainy morning and Bob was still asleep. He paced and paced, trying to work out a point on Emerson and Hawthorne. He looked down at his notes, then paced some more. The rain came down harder. He paced.

And then his vision rested on the material Trip had left on his desk, now sitting on top of the bed. He stared at the two folders marked "Thesis."

He suddenly became very still.

He went into the other bedroom and woke up Bob as gently as he could, taking hold of his hand and arm.

"Tell me again what Trip said that night."

"What? What's wrong?" Bob struggled to focus.

"Tell me again what Trip said that night. About something in the papers."

Bob tried to focus and tried to remember. "I think he said, 'I've nailed it. It's all right there, in the papers.'"

Marcus thought for a moment. "And those were his exact words?"

"I can't be a hundred percent sure, but ninety percent, yeah." Bob yawned.

"I need to look at something," Marcus said, leaving Bob to wonder what was going on.

Marcus went back to Trip's room. He looked at the bed and what was on it, the newspaper clippings and the thesis folders.

He realized he had only looked through the top few pages of each of the folders but had not searched them completely. He grabbed the first folder and sat down at the desk.

He looked carefully through every page in the folder. Notes, typed drafts, a few notecards. Everything familiar from the final thesis. Everything one would expect.

Marcus put the first folder back on the bed and grabbed the second, the thicker of the two. He sat back down at the desk. He hesitated for a moment. Then he slowly opened the folder and looked over each page carefully.

By now, Bob was standing in the doorway, watching him.

Under Trip's drafts and notes in the second folder were photocopies of some kind of transcript that Marcus had not seen before. He could tell from the typeface they had come from an old manual typewriter. At the top of the first page Trip had written "Edgerly, Schles" in red ink. Marcus recognized his handwriting. He slowed his breathing and then read the photocopies carefully.

They were about twelve pages of an analysis of Lincoln's rhetoric. Starting on the fifth page and continuing to the end were passages Trip had circled in red ink. The circled material amounted to perhaps four pages in total.

On the last page of photocopy, Trip had written "Echols" in the same red ink.

His heart started pounding, and he took a few more deep breaths. He reached for the copy of Deena Echols's book sitting in front of him. He had never moved Trip's books from the back of the desk. He had meant to take them back to the Harvard library but always forgot.

He hadn't opened any of the books, including Deena's, which he had read it when it first came out, about two years prior. He'd recommended it to Trip, and Trip had cited it in his thesis.

He pulled it out and flipped through the pages quickly. The corners of several pages toward the end of the book were turned down. He put the book next to the photocopies and read the turned-down pages, one by one.

The words in Deena's book were either exact copies of the words in the typescript or very close paraphrases.

Marcus closed his eyes for a moment, then turned around

to Bob.

"I know what Trip was worried about that day we met for lunch in Cambridge. And I know who might have wanted Trip dead."

25

Marcus showed Bob what he had found. "So what does this mean? What is 'Schles'?"

"The Schlesinger Library at Harvard. It has archives, papers, mostly by or about women. I remember Trip telling me he was going to check out some collections there for the thesis. I had to write a letter for him since they usually don't give access to undergraduates without special permission."

"And?"

Marcus stood up and started pacing again. "When Trip said 'it's in the papers,' he meant manuscripts, not newspapers."

Bob crinkled his brow. "So this means. . ."

"It means Deena Echols plagiarized material from someone's private papers. I'm guessing the typescript was a draft of something that was never published, written by someone named Edgerly."

"Does the name ring a bell?"

"No. Not at all. But who knows."

"Could it have been by accident?"

"Not this much material, no. A sentence or two, maybe."

"And Trip discovered it?"

"Yes."

"Could that lead to murder?" Bob looked incredulous.

"My hunch? Trip confronted Echols. He was just the type. His brother said he had a nose for scandal, corruption, and pushed things. Remember he called that reporter in Boston, told him to call David."

"You really think this could lead to his being killed?"

"Plagiarism, especially this much, this blatant, is the cardinal sin in academia. And that book was a big part of what got Deena tenure. At Harvard."

Bob was pensive. "Okay, so. She's a thief."

"A kind of thief. A fraud, certainly." Marcus was pacing up and down. "If Trip had exposed her, it would have been a scandal. Harvard would have to discipline her in some way. Maybe even fire her. The story would hit the press. Her reputation would be ruined."

Marcus walked past Bob to the other bedroom and started haphazardly dressing and shoving clothes into his bag.

"Where are you going?" Bob asked.

"We need to go back to town. I have to go to the Schlesinger library."

"Breakfast first," Bob said. "With decaf. You are really wound up."

26

As they left Miller's Cove, Marcus at the wheel, Bob was quiet until they drove out of Maine into New Hampshire.

"Marcus?"

"Hmm?"

"If she killed Trip she could kill you too. Maybe you have to go to the police with this."

Marcus hadn't thought of that. "You'll just have to protect me." He smiled.

"Marcus, I'm serious."

"One step at a time. I haven't done anything yet. First I have to be sure my theory is correct, that this is plagiarism of unpublished material. Then we can decide what to do."

Bob was relieved to hear "we."

"Okay. But I just found you. I don't want to lose you to some academic nut."

Marcus was moved. "I won't let that happen."

Bob had a skeptical look on his face.

"Really." Marcus smiled again, but for the first time since he heard about Trip's murder, he was worried.

When they got back to Cambridge, Marcus called the Schlesinger Library and asked about "the Edgerly papers," assuming they existed. They did, so he made an appointment to see them the next morning.

That evening, they walked to a little basement café off Harvard Square for dinner. They ordered, then Bob said, "tell me about Deena Echols."

"You met her at the memorial service. She's in the English department, and she's on the History/Lit committee. An expert on nineteenth-century American literature. The book Trip used was her second, on the relationship between literary themes and religion. She married a hot-shot lawyer. He was there too, at the service."

"You really think she's capable of murder?"

"I don't know her that well. We've been on a few committees together, that's about it. She was semi-friendly before she got tenure." Marcus thought for a moment. "She takes herself seriously. She has a high opinion of herself."

"I think you should go to the police with this."

"Maybe. First I need proof."

"Marcus, you're a professor, not a cop."

"I know. But cops are so sexy."

Bob scowled at the feeble attempt at a joke, and when their food came he changed the subject. He talked about the job interviews he had lined up, which ones sounded interesting, which ones didn't. Marcus listened, asked a few questions. His mind was still racing.

After dinner they strolled around aimlessly, looking into bookstore windows. That was something Marcus loved about Cambridge, there were so many bookstores and many of them stayed open in the evening.

Just before ten the next morning Marcus walked over to the Schlesinger Library. It stood on the corner of James Street and Brattle, near one of Marcus's favorite bakeries, on what was once the separate Radcliffe campus. It was red brick with columns, that peculiar Harvard style of architecture, at once simple and ostentatious. It had been named for the eminent historian Arthur Schlesinger Sr. and his wife, and it housed priceless books and manuscripts by and about women and the causes to which they had devoted themselves.

Marcus found the right room and was asked to wait. Soon boxes were brought to his table on a little cart. He dug in.

The first folder contained a biographical note about Dorothy Andrews Edgerly. She was born in Baltimore, the daughter of a physician. She was a cousin of the Warfields, the family that produced Wallis Simpson, the Duchess of Windsor, the woman who stole a king and rocked the British empire.

Something clicked into place. Marcus had heard that Trip's mother was from Baltimore. Perhaps there was a family connection that led Trip to the papers.

Edgerly had obtained her undergraduate degree in history from Radcliffe, spent a year at the Sorbonne in Paris, then returned and earned a PhD at the University of Wisconsin, where she taught as a lecturer for three years. She married an attorney and they moved to Boston, where she began independent research on nineteenth-century social movements and causes, including both the abolitionists and the defenders of slavery. She died of cancer before completing any of her work, donating her papers to Radcliffe. She had no children.

The other folders contained extensive notes and drafts. Edgerly had been very thorough, consulting material at libraries around the country, including the Library of Congress, the University of Virginia, and various other places in the South and West. There were also notes of interviews she had conducted with other historians and some descendants of important figures.

There was a folder marked "Lincoln."

Marcus glanced around the reading room, which was mostly empty. He closed his eyes. Then he got up, went to the men's room, and stared at himself in the mirror for a long time.

"What are you doing?" he said out loud to his image in the mirror.

But he knew what he was doing.

He wanted to know.

It was that simple. It was the impulse that had made him a diligent student for as long as he could remember, the impulse that had led him to graduate school and into academia, away from the world into which he had been born, or any other world for that matter. It was an impulse that, at the current moment, he wished he did not have. But he also knew he could not fight it.

He wanted to know.

He went back to his table and opened the folder, and there, along with some handwritten notes, was the typescript Trip had found, including pages Trip had not photocopied. It read like the draft of an article about Lincoln's rhetorical style, and it linked that style to both biblical themes and themes in the popular literature of the day.

And it was, without question, an argument Deena Echols had used without attribution, copying several passages verbatim. It made an astute comparison between Lincoln's use of biblical references and cadences and the same rhetorical devices as his opponents.

It was blatant plagiarism.

He looked up and let out a little laugh, and the clerk behind the desk shot him a disapproving glance. He photocopied a few pages Trip had not, including the biographical sketch of Edgerly, thanked the clerk, and left.

It was a bright, pleasant summer day, not too humid, and he walked over to the Cambridge Common, where George Washington had gathered troops during the Revolutionary War. He sat on a bench. A few children were playing while their parents sat and talked, as he imagined generations of children and parents had done before them. He watched them, envying their innocence.

"I'm fucked," he said out loud, and let out another little laugh.

27

Marcus spent the rest of the day aimlessly, walking in and out of shops and bookstores. He skipped lunch. He stopped at his office and sat at his desk for a while, doing nothing. He fiddled a bit with his new word processor, a Kaypro, and wondered if he'd ever figure out how it worked. He had a brief chat in the mailroom with a colleague about her summer adventures, but he wasn't really listening.

When he got back to Kirkland Street, Bob was napping, half naked. Marcus shed his clothes and joined him. Bob sat bolt upright.

"So?"

"So. It's definitely what I thought. Plagiarism. Clear cut. No question."

"Oh God. How could she think she'd get away with it?"

"Edgerly was obscure. She never published anything. She died young. I doubt very many people have ever looked at her papers. I don't know how Trip found his way to them."

"I see." Bob was thinking. "So now what?"

Marcus didn't know. He pulled Bob down. He wanted the sweet oblivion of sex.

After they both showered, Bob started making a big salad for dinner. Bread was baking in the oven.

"You have to go to the police."

Marcus pondered. "No. The police will immediately question Deena, and she'll stonewall. She'll admit nothing. Her husband will get her a high-priced lawyer. If she did it, she's smart enough to cover her tracks."

"Well, what then?"

"Maybe I can find more evidence."

"How? Marcus, if she is the killer, she's dangerous. And you just said she's smart. This is getting scary."

"I know."

"What if you just turn her in for the plagiarism?"

Marcus had thought about that. "Maybe, but the murder is what really matters. And I promised the family I'd find out what I could. The plagiarism case can wait. It's open and shut."

"Marcus—"

"I'll just see if I can find out where Deena was on the Fourth. For all we know she could have been anywhere. Paris. Santa Fe. Anywhere. Maybe she didn't do it."

"Marcus—"

"Let me do that much. Find out where she was. That's not dangerous."

Bob had his doubts, but he was beginning to know when Marcus was determined to do something.

They ate the salad, on which Bob had worked his usual wizardry. Then they settled in the living room with coffee, and Bob switched on the old black and white television. A movie was playing, a period piece, Bette Davis and Miriam Hopkins arguing over something or other.

"Oh good," Bob said, cuddling up to Marcus on the couch. "Let's watch Bette win."

"How do you know she'll win?"

"Bette always wins. Don't you know anything?"

28

Bob got up early for an interview and Marcus slept late. He roused himself, drank coffee and ate toast, as usual, and found a note from Bob, all in capital letters.

BE CAREFUL SHERLOCK!

Marcus smiled. This was new, he realized, having someone in his life who cared what happened to him. He hadn't felt that for a long time.

He considered his options.

He wouldn't confront Deena in her office. He'd invite her to lunch, say he needed her advice about something.

Advice about what?

His syllabus. It was mid-August, time to start preparing for the semester. What could be more natural?

Yes, that made sense. He'd invite her to lunch, ask her advice, casually work in mention of Trip. Throw a little shade. See if she flinched. He'd ask her how she spent the summer, if she'd gone anywhere interesting. All perfectly natural. One colleague casually catching up with another.

He felt some relief. He had a plan. He showered and dressed, reminding himself to call the maintenance department about the hot water, which always seemed to run out now that there were two of them.

He was shivering, but he smiled again. Two of them.

He walked over to his office and began organizing material for his fall classes. He would be teaching a graduate seminar on legal rhetoric, and a mid-level undergraduate lecture course, "American Political Thought," co-listed with the Government department. He had taught both before, so it would be a bit unusual to ask for advice.

He thought about how to get around that. He'd say he wasn't happy with the section of the course on the mid-nineteenth century, ask Deena what she'd assign, what she'd read as background.

Yes, that would work. That period was her specialty.

He wrote a short note to Deena and sent it through campus mail, then turned his attention to his work. Lying on his desk was a chapter from a graduate student's dissertation that he needed to read but had been avoiding since early summer because the student was floundering. He was writing on Thoreau and hadn't yet found a hook, a theme. What Marcus had read so far was a mess.

He dug in, forced himself to concentrate, wrote elaborate notes in the margins, then stuck the chapter in the student's mailbox.

Near the mailboxes Marcus ran into one of his senior colleagues, Arthur Banfield, who had always been friendly. Or as friendly as senior faculty got.

"Hello, how are you?" Banfield said. "Care for lunch?"

Marcus couldn't say no, even though he wanted to. Obligatory junior faculty deference, what one of his sardonic junior colleagues called "*politesse oblige.*"

They walked to the faculty club, Banfield chattering all the way and all through lunch about his research area,

American children's language, about which Marcus knew very little. Marcus nodded, tried to look interested.

"How's your own work going," Banfield finally asked as they were drinking coffee.

"Oh fine, fine. Concentrating right now on Emerson and Hawthorne, the unseen political implications of their writing." It wasn't really going fine, of course, but one did not tell the truth about such things. One never, ever admitted to trouble with one's scholarship. One of the rules, unspoken but crystal clear.

"Good, good," Banfield blandly replied.

After lunch Marcus was restless, so he decided to go for a swim. Blodgett pool was on Harvard's north campus, near the business school and some ugly modern apartments. He walked across the river, pausing for a while to watch the rowers—there always seemed to be rowers, whatever the weather—then changed in the locker room and swam a few laps, his lungs burning.

He got out of the pool, gasping a bit but feeling righteous for having exercised at all. All those baked goods Bob and Ruth made. He had to cut down.

By late afternoon he was back at Kirkland Street and Bob was cooking something spicy. Marcus kissed him on the neck. "How was the interview?"

"Oh, you know," Bob said, nonchalant. "I got it." He broke out in a big grin.

Marcus turned him around and hugged him. "You got it? Are you gonna take it?"

Bob was laughing now. "Yes. It sounds pretty good. He's a solo practitioner, mostly immigration work, and I'll be interviewing witnesses sometimes, that sort of thing. And the pay is good. Better than I expected."

"That's wonderful. We should go out. Celebrate."

"No," Bob said. "I want to stay in. Just you and me. I got a bottle of champagne."

"What are you cooking? It smells great."

"I have no idea what it is. I decided to experiment. It will somewhat resemble what they call dirty rice in New Orleans, only I'm using ground veal instead of ground beef."

"Well, dirty is always good," Marcus said, reaching for Bob's waist.

"None of that. Out, out of the kitchen."

Marcus washed his face, changed into a T-shirt and shorts, and sat down at his desk in the little alcove. He was really pleased for Bob, and giddily happy that he would be staying in town. Marcus didn't want him to leave.

Ever.

He turned his attention to his notes on Hawthorne.

After a while Bob walked into the bedroom, and Marcus could hear the closet door opening and closing. Then Bob walked into the alcove, stark naked.

"Um." Marcus feigned shock. "Are you trying to tell me something, young man?"

Bob smirked and grabbed his hand.

29

Over the next few weeks they settled into a different but pleasant rhythm. Bob's job started. He'd wake at 7:15, shower, eat breakfast, and leave just as Marcus was getting up. They kissed good-bye, and Bob told Marcus what to buy at the grocery store. Then Marcus drank some coffee, ate some toast or cereal, and sat at his desk for a few hours.

On the first day Bob went to work, Marcus's eyes settled on the memo he was writing for his fourth-year review, during which his colleagues would decide if they would add three years as an untenured associate professor to his contract. Before meeting Bob, Marcus had been slightly indifferent to the process, but now that Bob was in his life and planning on the Harvard Law School, Marcus desperately wanted the extra three years.

He had already published one book, and his teaching reviews were strong, so his chances were good, or so he had been told by some of his senior colleagues. The tricky part, he knew, was the statement about his future research plans. Marcus had drafted the memo describing his next book project, but he wasn't satisfied with it. Every so often he took it out and tinkered with it, adding a sentence here, subtracting one there, inserting a reference to something he had just read. He tried his best to make the project sound coherent, exciting, and original. Since he himself wasn't too sure it was exciting or original, it was rough going, but now he was determined to give it his best shot. It would be horrible if he had to leave Cambridge just as Bob started law school. God knows where he'd end up.

At noon most days he'd shower and dress and walk to the Square, grabbing lunch at the soup and salad place, or sometimes, if it was a nice day, buying a sandwich at Elsie's, the deli, and taking it to the steps of Memorial Church. He'd sit and watch the people in the Yard, his thoughts always returning to Trip and the memorial service. Then he'd go to his office, sort through mail, read a bit, work on his syllabi, tinker with his new computer. Around four he'd head home, stopping for groceries per Bob's instructions, and then he'd nap or clean the apartment.

An hour or so later, Bob would come home, change, and start cooking. Now that he was working he mostly wanted to eat in. Care packages full of baked goods regularly arrived from Danbury. After dinner they'd sometimes watch TV or take a walk if the weather was fine, sometimes going all the way to Steve's, the crowded ice cream place everyone loved.

On Saturday mornings they'd drive up to Miller's Cove, spending part of the day at the beach, eating out in the evening, sometimes stopping at the Veranda for a drink before or after dinner. It was mid-August but it was already getting a bit cool in Maine; fall was coming.

So this is domesticity, Marcus thought, and smiled to himself.

One Saturday as they were leaving Maineium's they ran into Lieutenant Fitzgerald. They exchanged pleasantries, and then Marcus asked him if there was any news.

Fitzgerald fidgeted. "I'm afraid not. We've done everything

we can think of, and we can't seem to get anywhere."

Marcus and Bob were downcast as they made their way to the beach.

"Maybe you need to tell him about Deena."

"Maybe. Let me meet with her first, see if I get anything. She won't know I'm on the case, and she might reveal something."

Bob frowned but kept quiet.

They drove back to Cambridge late Sunday. On Monday afternoon at his office, Marcus's phone rang. It was Trip's father.

"I'm going to be in town tomorrow. Could we meet for lunch?"

They met at the Harvard Club in Boston. Marcus didn't even know the place existed; he thought everything Harvard was in Cambridge. He put on a coat and tie and caught the T, sweating.

The club building reminded Marcus of the Schlesinger Library, that weird combination of simple and pretentious. He told the maître d' he was expected by Mr. Howard and was led past table after table of distinguished-looking men, and a few women, clearly all business types. The dean of the faculty was at one table and seemed surprised to see Marcus there. He nodded and Marcus smiled, enjoying the moment. He might have been the first assistant professor ever to set foot in the place. He noticed David Howard at another table, deep in a conversation with someone Marcus didn't recognize, although he looked somewhat familiar. The conversation was intense and David did not even notice Marcus as he walked by.

Mr. Howard was at a table at the back, near a window, drinking a martini. That was still new to Marcus, all this drinking. It started in graduate school at Princeton, when he'd noticed almost the entire faculty drank at lunch, at dinner, before dinner, after dinner. It was the same at Harvard. He wondered how anyone got anything done.

Howard rose and shook Marcus's hand.

"Would you like one?"

"No, thanks. Mineral water, please," he told the hovering waiter.

"I'll have another, Jack," Howard said. Jack nodded and disappeared.

Marcus considered what it took to get to a place in life where you drank martinis at lunch and knew the name of the waiters at a private club. He and Howard exchanged pleasantries and ordered their lunches. Marcus waited for the inevitable question.

"So, are you still looking into things? Any progress?"

Marcus wanted to be careful. "I found something that might be a lead, but I don't want to say too much. It may come to nothing."

"I see. Do let us know. We've given up hope that the local police will get anywhere. They seem to have given up too. We're really hoping you can help us."

"I'll do what I can."

There was an awkward pause. By now David had noticed Marcus and cast several nervous glances in his direction.

After an awkward pause, Marcus said, "I hope this isn't too personal, but I can't imagine there's anything more difficult than losing a child."

Mr. Howard looked startled. Marcus hoped he hadn't spoken out of turn.

"No, nothing worse. It's been awful for us all, but especially Trip's mother, and David. David is taking it very hard, probably the hardest of all. We're a bit worried about him."

This was a surprise. Marcus knew from his own experience how fraught sibling relationships could be, and he assumed there must have been some tension in that family, given their social position, what with Trip coming out as proudly gay. After all, David was doing what had been expected for generations; Trip was not.

Marcus cleared his throat. "May I ask you a question?"

"Of course. Anything."

"I'm trying to reconstruct Trip's work on his thesis, to see if anything there might have created a problem for him. In his research he consulted some unpublished papers. In one of the Harvard manuscript collections." Mr. Howard was listening distractedly.

"The papers were the work of a woman named Dorothy Andrews Edgerly. Did Trip by any chance mention this? Does the name ring a bell?"

Howard seemed to be thinking and took a large gulp of his second martini. "Yes, now that you mention it. Dorothy was a cousin of my wife's, from Baltimore. She died young. She was an historian, trained somewhere out west."

For Harvard and families like the Howards, Wisconsin was the west, part of that vast unknown region beyond the Eastern Seaboard. Marcus suppressed a smile.

"My wife suggested to Trip that he look at her papers when he told us about his thesis topic. Why do you ask?"

"I wondered how Trip knew the papers were there." That seemed to satisfy Howard.

After coffee they walked out of the club together and shook hands.

Howard had a limo waiting.

"Can I drop you somewhere?"

"Thanks, no." Again Marcus suppressed a smile. He couldn't remember ever riding in a limo.

30

Two days later, the phone rang around ten in the morning while Marcus was working at home.

"Marcus, Deena Echols. Sorry I haven't responded sooner, I've just been swamped." Everyone at Harvard was constantly swamped. She invited him to lunch the next day at the faculty club, assuming he'd be free. "I'll meet you at one."

That night at dinner Bob once again urged him to go to the police, and Marcus once again resisted.

"Let me just see how this goes," he said.

The Harvard Faculty Club on Quincy Street was of a piece with much of the campus. Both stately and shabby, old wood and old furniture, mediocre food. Marcus met Deena in one of the lounges, where she was chatting with an eminent economist who had advised several presidents.

They all went into the main dining room after filling in the cards that would discreetly charge them for their lunches. Nothing so vulgar as money ever changed hands at the faculty club. The economist excused himself. Marcus wondered how much his very elegant summer suit had cost.

Marcus followed Deena to a table and began the conversation with his syllabus, the excuse he'd used to bring them together. Deena looked bored but made a few suggestions about what he had been assigning. Marcus dutifully wrote them down. Their food arrived.

"How has your summer been?" he asked as nonchalantly as he could manage.

"Oh, you know. Too many projects, too little time."

"Did you get away at all?"

"We spent a week with Jordan's family on the Cape. And you?"

"Well, I've been going back and forth to Miller's Cove in Maine, which I quite like. Except that I was there over the Fourth, when Trip Howard was murdered."

Marcus tried not to look at Deena too intently but watched for her reaction. He thought he detected a tightening around her eyes, a slight blanching of her face.

"Oh, my. I hadn't realized you were there for the murder. That must have been dreadful."

"Yes, it was."

"Do you know, are the police getting anywhere? Such a strange story."

"I don't know. Nothing's been in the papers. They talked to me, of course, but I couldn't tell them much," Marcus paused. "Where did you spend the Fourth?"

"Oh, we were here. Jordan couldn't get away from work. We had a few people over. Very low key."

So she had an alibi, and witnesses. Or at least that was her story. Marcus pressed on. "Trip had come to talk to you about his thesis, hadn't he?"

"Yes, twice. Or maybe it was three times. Smart young man. A bit headstrong, but they are at that age, aren't they? And I gather he was from a very prominent family."

"The Howards, yes. You know he once told me they were distantly related to the dukes of Norfolk?" Deena seemed impressed. "His father is on our Board of Overseers. Or the Corporation, I forget which." It was the first time Marcus had ever referred to anything having to do with Harvard as "our." He continued matter-of-factly. "While I was up there they had me to their house in Kennebunkport, and I just had lunch with Mr. Howard. Naturally they're still very keen on finding out what happened."

More tightening around the eyes. "Naturally," she said.

Marcus allowed a pensive look to cross his face, and stopped asking questions. He didn't want to push his luck.

"Well, I must dash," Deena said, standing up. "Make those changes to your syllabus, I'm sure it will go fine." And with that, she was gone.

Her departure was abrupt, and a little rude, Marcus thought. Perhaps he'd rattled her. Or perhaps it was just a senior faculty member deciding she'd spent enough time on someone who didn't matter.

That night, over lamb chops, Marcus recounted the lunch to Bob.

"Well, clearly," Bob said, "she wasn't going to confess to murder over lunch."

Marcus went on as though Bob hadn't spoken. "I have to find out who was with her on the Fourth. Check out her story."

"Or the police could do it," Bob said hopefully.

"No, I can't talk to the police yet. Like I said, she'll clam up, lawyer up."

Bob admitted that was undoubtedly true. "But how can you find out who was invited to a casual thing?"

"Oh, honey. This is Harvard. Deena is a rising star. Invitations matter. And people talk."

Bob shook his head. "I'll never understand academia."

"Well," Marcus said, "you understand me."

"More and more." Bob leaned over and kissed him. "So what are you in the mood for?"

"Mmm. Ice cream and sex. Not necessarily in that order."

"Well, there happens to be a half gallon of mint chocolate chip in the freezer."

"And are there any cute gay men around?"

"I'll walk to the Square, see if I can find any."

After the ice cream, Bob turned to Marcus and said he had an idea. Marcus was kissing the back of his neck.

"Not now."

"Sex sex sex. You only want me for my body."

Later, lying happily in bed, Marcus said, "so tell me your idea."

"Let's go down to Danbury on Saturday, ask Dad for advice about the case. We can talk to him off the record, and he might think of something we haven't."

Marcus wondered if Bob hoped his father would tell them to turn things over to police.

"Good idea," he said. "More borscht."

31

Ruth served the same lunch they had had before, but this time Jake was there. Both parents seemed delighted to see them, and the borscht was even better than Marcus remembered it.

"What is in this borscht?" he asked.

"Oh, I can't tell you that," Ruth laughed. "Family secret."

"Dad, after lunch can we talk?" Bob asked. "We need a legal opinion, off the record." His parents glanced at each other.

"Nothing wrong, I hope," Ruth said.

"No, no, just something Marcus is dealing with at the university."

"Sure. Of course," Jake said. "Just let me make a couple of calls."

Ruth said she had a tennis game. She announced that that night they were taking Marcus and Bob to a new restaurant they'd been wanting to try. "It's supposed to be wonderful. Best fish in Connecticut, one of the reviews said. Which is saying something."

Bob and Marcus cleaned up from lunch, and by then Jake was ready to talk. They settled in the den.

Bob began. "One of Marcus's students was murdered up

in Maine, in Miller's Cove. His name was Trip Howard. I was sharing that house with him. He was shot. On the Fourth."

"Trip?"

"Addison Cornell Howard the Third."

Jake Abramson shook his head and smiled. "Gentiles."

"Dad, please."

"Sorry. I hadn't heard about the murder, and of course it's shocking. Why didn't you tell us about it? It must have been awful."

"I didn't really know Trip, we were just sharing a house for the summer, by chance. I didn't want to worry you." He left out the part about how he and Trip had been briefly involved years before.

Marcus filled in the rest of the story as Jake listened carefully.

"So you're sure about the plagiarism? No ambiguity?"

"No. None at all."

"And you think that might have led to . . ."

"Murder." Marcus said. "It's possible. If this plagiarism were made known, it would ruin her."

Bob spoke up. "I'm worried about Marcus getting too deep into this. If Deena killed Trip, she's dangerous. Shouldn't Marcus turn this over to the police?"

Marcus explained his reasons for not wanting to do that.

"It's true," Jake agreed. "She'll get a high-priced lawyer and say nothing. Her husband is well known. Word is he's on the list for a judgeship, maybe even the State Supreme Court. And if the police get involved, they'll bring in the FBI. It's would be an interstate crime."

Marcus and Bob let that sink in.

"So yes, it makes sense to check out the alibi, if—and it's a big if—if you can do it discreetly," Jake said.

Bob frowned. It was the opposite of what he wanted to hear. His plan had backfired.

"Maybe I can help a bit," Jake continued. "I know someone in the Massachusetts State Police. He used to work down here, and I helped him once, a long time ago. I'll ask him to find out if this professor or her husband own a weapon. Or at least if they own one that's registered."

"That would be very helpful," Marcus said. "Thank you."

"But listen. Once you check out the alibis, Bob is right. I wouldn't go much further. Go to your contact in the Miller's Cove police and tell him everything. Let him take it from there."

"Good advice," Bob said.

Jake excused himself to do some work. Marcus and Bob went out to the back yard and took lounge chairs under a large surviving elm tree that provided just the right amount of shade. It was warm, but there was a nice breeze.

"So how long have you all been in this house?" Marcus asked.

"Since I was born. They moved in just a few days before. I came a bit early. Mom used to joke that she almost lost me amidst all the boxes."

Marcus looked around at the flower beds, the well-tended lawn. "It must have been a lovely place to grow up."

"It was. Until puberty hit."

"And then?"

"And then, I was a handful. I had the hots for Gary Litwin in eighth grade."

"Ah. Whatever happened to old Gary?"

"He played football at Penn. Just got married."

"Is he still hot?"

"God, is he ever. But they moved to Utah. He took some

job with a chemical company."

"Ah well" Marcus said, feigning sympathy.

"And what were you doing in eighth grade, hmm?"

"Studying."

Bob laughed.

Just then, Ruth came home, flushed from tennis, and joined them. "Was Dad able to help?"

"Yes and no," Bob said.

"Definitely, yes." Marcus paused. "A student of mine, an acquaintance of Bob's, was murdered this summer."

"Oh God," Ruth said. They told her just a bit of the story, and she listened intently. "How awful, for both of you."

"Well," Bob said, "yes. Awful. But it did bring us together." He reached over for Marcus's hand.

Never in a million years could Marcus imagine taking a boyfriend's hand in front of his own mother. He wondered what percentage of gay men in America would say the same thing, especially now that so many were sick and dying, but his musings were cut short when a thunderclap, followed by a sudden rain, chased them into the house.

Bob and Marcus took naps, Ruth baked some cookies for them to take back to Cambridge.

Dinner that night at the new restaurant was wonderful, as advertised. Everyone was relaxed, and Jake and Ruth told funny stories about their Danbury neighbors, including the woman who was on her fifth marriage but always kept the house in the divorce settlements.

They all slept late on Sunday morning. Ruth made blueberry pancakes for brunch, and then they sat in the den reading *The New York Times*. Thunderstorms were predicted for later in the day, so Bob suggested they drive back sooner rather than later. It was getting darker by the minute.

"Probably a good idea," Jake said.

Marcus and Bob showered and said their good-byes, with the obligatory package of baked goods tucked under Bob's arm. Marcus said very little as they drove north, and finally Bob asked him what he was thinking.

"How lucky you are."

32

It was almost Labor Day, and Marcus started working on his courses in earnest. The weather was still warm, but a slight chill in the air reminded everyone that this was New England. Summer was short.

Every year the Saturday came when the arriving freshmen moved into their dorms in Harvard Yard. Marcus always made it a point to walk to his office that day and watch them, the proud parents carrying boxes, the new students impatient for their parents to be gone. *The Harvard Crimson* published something they called the "Configuide," a well-written and funny review of courses that was always on sale that day.

Marcus would buy a copy to see what they had said about him and his colleagues. That year he was described as an "elegant" lecturer whose courses were "usually entertaining." He smiled. After his first year he had been described as "a bit wobbly," with the guide going on to say, "but what else can you expect from someone who studied at Princeton and went to a land-grant University?" Marcus took it in stride and concentrated on not wobbling. He knew what they meant; he sometimes made things too gray. Undergraduates wanted black and white.

Tinkering with his syllabi, getting his lecture notes

organized, meeting with incoming and returning graduate students, were all things Marcus enjoyed. For as long as he could remember, the beginning of the school year, that slight nip in the air while it was still sunny and mild, was the time he loved best.

He and Bob spent weekends in Miller's Cove through the end of September. Farther north than Boston, autumn was definitely in the air, especially when the breeze came off the ocean.

One Sunday afternoon while Bob napped, Marcus walked along the shore, stopped and finally sat down on the bench under the awning where Trip had been killed. He stared out at the ocean trying to imagine someone standing there and firing a gun at Trip point-blank. He listened to the waves, watched the gulls flying around. Hard to envision such a cold-blooded crime amidst so much beauty, so much peace. Except of course it had been the Fourth of July, so not quiet.

At Kirkland Street that evening, Marcus made a list of people who might have been invited to Deena's house on the Fourth. He was guessing, but he did know some of the people Deena considered friends, at least a few of them well enough to engineer a casual meeting, ask them about their summers, what they did over the Fourth. He realized he needed to see them as soon as possible. Before long, talk of the summer would seem strange, out of place.

Classes started. His undergraduate class was crowded, about fifty students, and it met, incongruously, in a chemistry lab. The graduate seminar had enrolled seven. Teaching grad students as a junior faculty member could be tricky. They were there to work with the famous senior faculty members, not with a lowly assistant professor, against whom they judged themselves. Marcus understood that, but at that particular moment there was no senior faculty member in his specialty, so they had to settle for him. Some of them were a handful.

One by one, Marcus invited some of Deena's possible alibis to lunch or to meet for coffee. His gut told him the most likely candidates were the younger, untenured faculty in her department or in closely allied departments or programs. They were likely trying to curry favor with her, and she would like that; he was sure she was enjoying her newfound power as a senior faculty member.

When he met them, Marcus would talk about discovering Miller's Cove over the summer and mention the horrible murder of one of his students there on the Fourth. Some had heard the story of the murder, some had not. He'd say something about how crowded things were in resorts on the Fourth, or how odd it was that Americans celebrated independence with a barbecue, or some such, and then casually ask them what they did that day. Sometimes he'd find a way to bring Deena's name into the conversation and see how they reacted.

At his fifth such meeting, he caught a break. Geoff Marston was an assistant professor of English, ambitious—ruthlessly so, some said—and determined to earn tenure from within. He'd earned his doctorate at Cambridge and spoke with the slightest English accent even though he grew up in Minneapolis.

"Oh, Deena and Jordan had me over," he said when Marcus brought up the Fourth.

"Ah, nice. Was it a barbecue?"

"An open house. Deena called, said to stop by any time after noon."

"Was it crowded?" Marcus hoped that wasn't too leading

a question.

"Not very, at least not when I was there. Suzanne was there, a few others." Suzanne was a mutual friend, a young historian. The three of them had been on a committee together and had commiserated about how boring and useless the committee was. Marcus didn't probe further, but called Suzanne as soon as he got back to his office, inviting her to lunch. They met three days later. He told the usual Miller's Cove story. Suzanne had read about the murder and commiserated.

"Yes, it was awful," Marcus said. "How was your holiday?"

"I was in town. Deena had a small party. Or I should say, Jordan did."

Marcus snapped to attention. "What do you mean?"

"By the time I got there Deena had excused herself. Apparently she had a migraine and needed to lie down. She went upstairs."

"Oh, too bad. I didn't know Deena suffered from migraines."

"Yes, it cast a pall over the party, since most of the people there were Harvards. Jordan did his best, but it was a bit awkward."

"Who else was there?"

Suzanne mentioned a few names.

Marcus's mind raced. If Deena had left the party at, say, three o'clock or four or even five, she'd have easily been able to drive to Miller's Cove. So the timing worked. He wondered about her house. Was there a way to slip out unnoticed and get into a car? Was there a garage, an alley? Could she have left the house through a back door and walked down the block or around the corner to wherever she had left her car? Marcus realized he'd have to look over the layout of the house, at least on the outside.

That night he told Bob about what he'd heard. Bob was intrigued.

"I got Deena's address from a faculty roster. I'm going to walk over there tomorrow, see what I can see."

"No," Bob said. "I'll go. Deena doesn't know me. How would you explain what you were doing there?"

The house was off Brattle Street, not too far from where Bob was working, and he walked over on his lunch hour. Luckily it was a nice day, so he could always say he was just stretching his legs. He bought a bottle of iced tea as a prop.

It was a narrow house on a medium-sized lot, and there was indeed a garage in the back, opening to an alley. There was also a small lawn and a back door.

Bob closed his eyes and sighed. "Oh God," he said out loud on the way back to his office. He dutifully reported all this to Marcus when he got home from work.

"So she could have slipped out," Marcus said.

"Yes, it's possible. Now it's time to call the police."

"First let's see if your father found out anything about the gun."

They called Danbury that night, and Jake said he had contacted his acquaintance in the Massachusetts police but hadn't heard back. He was clearly interested to hear about the migraine and the layout of the house. He said he'd call his police contact again in the morning.

Meanwhile, Marcus had set up a lunch for the next day with one of the people Suzanne had mentioned, the one he knew best, Amy Bernstein from the Religion Department. She confirmed Suzanne's story; Deena had excused herself "around midafternoon," Amy said, adding an important detail that Suzanne had left out: Jordan, she said, had gone upstairs a few times to check on Deena.

That night he told Bob what Amy had said.

"So if Deena really was upstairs . . ." Bob mused.

Marcus finished the sentence. "She couldn't have gotten to Miller's Cove."

Bob was thinking. "Unless Jordan knew what she was planning and went up to an empty bedroom."

Marcus stared at him; he hadn't thought of that. "Which would mean . . ."

"Which would mean that Jordan would be an accessory to murder."

They were sitting in stunned silence when the phone rang. It was Jake. Bob handed the phone to Marcus.

"Jordan Echols owns a pistol. A Beretta 92FS. What kind of gun killed your victim?"

"I don't know," Marcus said, "but I'll try to find out." He swallowed hard.

33

They stayed up late into the night. Bob was adamant that it was time to turn everything over to the Miller's Cove police. Marcus still wasn't sure. He was pacing the living room while Bob watched him from couch.

"I think I should talk to Deena again."

"Marcus—"

"She's looking more and more guilty. Any scrap of information I can get out of her before she's an official suspect could be important."

Bob was weary, and worried. He wanted sleep. But he could see that Marcus had that determined look again. He stood up and took hold of Marcus by the shoulders.

"You have to talk to Fitzgerald. At this point you could be charged with interfering with an investigation, or withholding evidence, or whatever they call this kind of thing."

Marcus saw that Bob was frightened. "Just one more lunch with Deena. I'll be careful."

Bob said nothing more. He went into the bedroom and closed the door. He was in bed when Marcus joined him a few minutes later and took his hand.

"I know you're worried. I won't be confrontational. I'll just see if I can get any new morsel of information. I'll be really careful, I promise."

Bob rolled away from him.

The next day a fretful Marcus taught his class in the morning, as usual, then went to his office and made two calls. The first was to Deena's office. She didn't pick up, so he left a message on the machine, saying he wondered if it would be all right to send her a few pages he was writing on Emerson to see if he was getting things right. "I'll send them through campus mail. Please call me when you've had a chance to read them, and thanks in advance."

The second call was to Lieutenant Fitzgerald. They exchanged pleasantries, and then Marcus asked if there was any progress in the case.

"Unfortunately, no."

"Too bad," Marcus said, and waited a bit. "Can you tell me what kind of gun killed Trip?"

"Why do you ask?"

"Curiosity, mostly. I'm trying to get a full picture of what happened. I don't see how someone could get shot like that outside, in a public place, on a holiday, with no witnesses."

"It was noisy, there was loud music coming from some of the houses, fireworks, lots of loud drunk people stumbling around."

"I see."

"And Howard was shot with a Beretta. A model that has a silencer. He probably just looked like a drunk slumped on a bench."

34

A Beretta with a silencer. Marcus stood up, grabbed his jacket, and headed for Harvard Square. For the first time, he was really frightened. Part of him, he realized, had been hoping all along that he'd been sending himself on a wild goose chase.

He walked and walked, telling himself he hadn't put himself or Bob in real danger. A wind was blowing, and he pulled up the collar of his corduroy jacket, remembering it was the same jacket he'd worn for his lunch with Trip. That seemed like years ago, though had only been a few short months.

A chill went down his spine. What if Deena heard he was asking questions about her party on the Fourth? He hadn't even thought of that—until now. He tried to reconstruct every conversation he'd had about the party. Was he casual enough? Did the questions sound natural? And, most important of all, would anyone have reported back to Deena?

He decided there was little danger of that. He'd been careful, and no one had seemed surprised or annoyed by his questions. It was just the usual Harvard junior faculty banter, who did what when. He hoped.

But he needed advice. He needed to confide in someone,

check his thinking with someone who wasn't involved, who didn't know Deena or Trip. As he walked, he thought of one of the faculty members he had worked with at Princeton, Fred Tucker, one of the few who had abundant common sense. He called him at home late that afternoon from Kirkland Street.

Tucker was a genial man in his early sixties who taught literary theory; Marcus had taken his seminar. On occasion Tucker would have graduate students over to his house on a Friday evening, serving white wine and gossip. If Harvard gossip was intense, it was nothing compared to that at Princeton, a smaller, more insular place, with no surrounding city as an escape valve. Marcus tried to avoid it all as much as he could, which was close to impossible. Grad students had no choice but to live in the faux-Gothic Graduate College, which meant living an almost monastic life in a petri dish of competition and insecurity.

Tucker was happy to hear from him, and they caught up. Then Marcus got to the business at hand.

"Fred, I need your advice about something. Not over the phone. Could I come down to Princeton, or could we perhaps meet in Manhattan?"

"Yes, sure. Molly and I will be in New York next weekend, in fact. I'll have some time on Friday afternoon."

Marcus thanked him, and they made arrangements to meet in the Oak Bar at the Plaza. Marcus decided not to tell Bob why he was going to New York. He'd make up an excuse of some sort. He knew he'd feel guilty about lying, but he also knew Bob was worried enough as it was.

The next day, Marcus had his regular therapy appointment. Since they had started meeting again in September, he had kept Gary up to date on what was happening, both in his pursuit of the murder case and in his relationship with Bob, which, he told Gary, felt more and more comfortable and secure. But now that he knew about the gun, he talked to Gary for the first time about fear, and about whether he was pushing things too far.

"Why do you think you don't want to turn it all over to the police? It certainly sounds as if this suspect could be dangerous. Why would you want to take chances with her?"

Marcus thought for a moment. "I don't really know."

"Well, find out," Gary replied. It was the kind of thing he often said, making matters sound simple when they were anything but, or so it seemed to Marcus.

Marcus was thinking. "Maybe in some way I feel responsible for what happened to Trip. If only he had told me what was happening at that first lunch after graduation, maybe . . ."

"Well, he chose not to. You made yourself available," Gary said.

Yes, that was true. So maybe he couldn't let go because it was Trip's murder that brought him to Bob, that brought them together. "Maybe on some weird level I worry if I give up the case it would mean losing Bob."

Gary said nothing. He had the look on his face that Marcus had come to realize meant, "That's an interesting thought."

"Or maybe I feel an obligation to the family."

"Do you think you want the family's approval? Rich, connected Harvard family, you a working-class kid from the Midwest." They had spent a lot of time early on talking about approval and disapproval.

"Maybe so."

"Or do you have something against this woman who just

earned tenure? Resentment? Jealousy?"

Marcus admitted to wondering the same thing.

"Or do you think," Gary ventured, "you might be using this case to avoid your own work?"

That was a surprise, something that hadn't occurred to Marcus. "I don't know. I have to think about that one."

"Well, think hard, because clearly you're getting in deeper and deeper. You are preoccupied with the case. Be careful."

"Are you telling me to let it go?"

"No. You know this by now. You have to make your own decisions. But I think you do need to consider all this carefully. Murder is nothing to fool around with."

35

That night the chair of Marcus's department had his usual beginning-of-the-term open house, something Marcus dreaded every year.

He debated with himself whether to take Bob but knew he would never be able to live with himself if he didn't. Some of his colleagues knew that Marcus was gay; others probably assumed. Some were oblivious. And one or two were homophobic. Manfred McAlister, an extremely conservative political philosopher who studied the Greeks, had made a crack at one department meeting about somebody's "boyfriend." It was not said in a friendly manner. Marcus didn't understand how someone who studied the Greeks could be homophobic, but there it was. At another meeting Karl Halperin, who studied African literature, made a joke about AIDS.

The chair, Sam Cochran, who studied the history and culture of Eastern Europe, lived in a gargantuan house that he and his wife had renovated with her family's money. She had a thick, though very genteel, Southern accent; her family had been prominent in South Carolina for generations, almost certainly back to slaveholding days. She and Sam had four children ranging in age from six to fourteen, and, of course, a live-in, African American nanny *cum* maid. At a meeting the previous year when graduate students complained about paltry financial aid and low academic salaries, Sam had tried to joke by saying "there's a simple solution. Marry money." Nobody laughed.

Bob could tell that Marcus was in a foul mood as they finished dressing. "What's the matter? It's just a party."

"I know. But I hate these things."

"Why?"

"Everything that's going to be on display. Old money. Power. Heterosexuality."

Bob laughed. Marcus poured himself a double whiskey and swallowed it in two quick gulps.

"Oh my, you really are dreading this, aren't you? I don't have to go with you, you know."

"It's not you, it's them. And it's 1985, not 1965. No skulking."

Sam's house wasn't far from Marcus's apartment, and they set out on foot. It was a lovely evening with a gentle breeze. Marcus had purposely arranged to arrive late, when the place was already crowded. In addition to the faculty, the chair always invited most of the department's graduate students.

Sam greeted Marcus at the door.

"Sam, this is Bob Abramson."

To Marcus's surprise, Sam didn't so much as blink. "Lovely to meet you. Come in. The bar is over there, in the dining room, and the kids are somewhere, circulating with food."

Good for him, Marcus thought happily.

As they made their way to the bar, Marcus smiled or nodded or said hello to the people he knew, introducing Bob to those closest by. As he watched their reactions, he noticed that the faculty wives were the most comfortable with Bob, the most welcoming. His colleagues, on the other hand, were a mixed bag, as he expected. McAlister, of course, glared at Marcus and moved to the other side of the living room, but apart from that, no one was overtly hostile or unfriendly. There were just a few of those tiny, subtle signs of discomfort that every gay man in America knew by heart.

They got themselves drinks and grabbed some canapés from one of the trays. Julia Cochran, the hostess, found them and greeted Marcus. She was wearing a gorgeous blue silk dress and a strand of pearls that hung down to her midriff. She was the kind of woman that at her age the world called handsome.

Marcus introduced Bob, and Julia shook his hand, smiling. "Lovely to meet you. Please make yourself at home. Do excuse me, I need to check something in the kitchen."

"That was the Alabama two-step," Bob said after she left.

"The what?"

"Smile, greet, leave. A friend of mine at Brown who grew up in Birmingham told me that's what people in the South do when they feel uncomfortable, mostly around Black people. They aren't impolite, but they get away as quickly as possible."

"Well, I suppose it's better than lynching," Marcus said.

A graduate student he knew came up to them and immediately began talking about his dissertation. Marcus nodded, Bob feigned interest. When he left, another graduate student approached, a woman. Same routine.

"Is that how they all are? Obsessed?" Bob asked.

Marcus sighed. "Yes."

"Were you like that?"

"Of course not. I was and always have been perfect. You know that."

Marcus had been drinking another scotch, and Bob could tell he was getting tipsy.

"I think I better take you home, Mr. Perfect."

"Please. Yes. Let's get out of here."

Marcus thanked Sam at the door, and Sam said, "Fine, fine. Glad you could come. Very nice to meet you, Bob. Please come again."

Fresh air helped sober Marcus up a bit.

"So that's Harvard."

"Well, a piece of it. Interesting that the wives were the most friendly."

"Yes. They're outsiders here, in a way. So they understand, at least on some level. Was Princeton like this?"

"Smaller. More real friendliness. But I was single, so who knows. Did you hate it?"

"No, not at all. I love making the elite sweat a little."

At that Marcus relaxed a little. Back home Bob made him drink coffee, and they polished off yet another sponge cake.

"If you keep baking like this," Marcus said, "I'm going to get huge."

"Then I'll leave you for one of those cute graduate students."

"The hell you will," Marcus said, and grabbed him. He promised himself to swim more often.

36

On the appointed day Marcus took the train to New York for his meeting with Fred Tucker. He got to the Plaza a bit early, settled in, and ordered a seltzer. For a moment he wondered what the hell he was doing in a fancy bar in a fancy hotel in Manhattan, lying to his boyfriend, investigating a murder.

Fred arrived right on time, greeted Marcus warmly, and ordered white wine. Marcus smiled; he remembered that Fred had always served white wine at those Friday nights in Princeton.

"What brings you to town?" Marcus asked.

"A wedding. A cousin of Molly's, tomorrow, at the Pierre."

"Nice." Marcus couldn't think of what else to say.

"I actually like most of Molly's family. It will be fine. I like them more than my own relatives, in fact." Fred took a sip of his wine. "So what can I help you with?"

"I think a senior colleague might have murdered a student."

Fred looked thunderstruck. Marcus told him the whole story, from the beginning. When he had finished, Fred literally whistled. People stared.

"That's quite a tale."

"I know. So what do I do?"

Fred considered. "One, you report the plagiarism to the dean and let the University wheels turn. Two, you tell the police everything you know. So far, the case against this woman is completely circumstantial. It looks damning, yes, but there's nothing definitive. Maybe she really did have a migraine. Maybe the gun is a coincidence. Lots of people own guns, and if the husband is a high-powered lawyer, as you say, maybe he sometimes deals with unsavory characters, feels he needs protection. And there's crime in Cambridge."

Marcus hadn't considered either possibility.

"Get out of it. You do have a professional obligation on the plagiarism. You can't ignore it. Let the administration deal with it. And let the police deal with this woman, one way or another."

Marcus fiddled with his seltzer. "That certainly makes a lot of sense."

"But you're not convinced, I can tell."

"I don't know. The whole thing has me a bit crazy."

"Listen to me," Fred said. "Protect yourself. Get on with your career. Live your life with this young man you've found."

Marcus felt a stab of longing. Yes, Bob. Bob was what was important.

They rose to leave and walked out to Fifth Avenue together.

"Be sensible, Marcus. Don't be an idiot," Fred said as they shook hands.

Marcus thanked him and watched him walk down Fifth. Checking his watch, he realized that if he took a cab he could catch the 5:30 train for Boston. It would get in late, but he didn't care, he wanted to go home, he wanted to sleep in his own bed, next to Bob. The therapy appointment, Fred's advice, everything was a jumble in his head.

He made the train with five minutes to spare and settled into his seat. He bought a turkey sandwich and a cup of coffee from the dining car, then looked out the window until he felt sleepy and dozed off. He made it back to Kirkland Street before midnight.

"It's me, not Deena Echols," he called.

Bob was in the bedroom, reading. "Very funny. What happened?"

Marcus had said he was going down to look at some manuscripts at the New York Public Library. "There wasn't really anything there. Wild goose chase."

"Ah, too bad."

Marcus undressed but didn't have the energy even to brush his teeth. He woke late the next morning to brunch, lox and bagels Bob had bought the day before. Bob told him about the case he was working on, a family from Guatemala that was facing deportation. He could tell Marcus wasn't really listening.

"What's up? You seem distracted."

"I'm sorry. I guess the trip yesterday took it out of me."

"And you're still thinking about the case and what to do, aren't you?" They hadn't been together more than a few months, but Bob was already reading his thoughts.

"Yes," Marcus said.

"So . . . what?"

"I don't know. I'm not going to do anything yet. Really, I'd like to forget the whole thing."

Bob looked relieved. "Good."

"I have an idea," Marcus said. "Let's drive up to the beach. We can stay at one of the inns. I'm sure we can find a room, it's off-season. It'll be a pretty drive, with the leaves changing."

"Um, sure."

"I'll call now. You pack us a bag."

37

They were on the road by noon, and they both felt a bit giddy. The leaves were indeed beautiful, more and more so as they drove north. They checked into the Hilltop Inn, where Marcus had stayed in July, then had a late lunch at Maineium's. The town wasn't empty, but it was much less crowded and more relaxed.

They went for a long walk on the beach. It was chilly but bearable. Back to the inn in the late afternoon, they made love.

Yes, this is love, not just sex, Marcus thought as he buried his face in Bob's chest. *And my life has changed.*

Sunday morning was bright with sunshine. They went to Maineium's for brunch, then for another walk on the beach. It was warmer than Saturday, and after the walk they sat on one of the benches at the entrance to the beach. The awning had been taken down for the season.

They stayed quite a while, listening to the waves and the gulls. Bob rested his head on Marcus's shoulder and seemed like he was dozing off.

"Bobby."

"Hmm."

"I love you."

"Stop talking dirty."

"I mean it. I love you. If we could, I'd ask you to marry me."

Bob sat up. "What's today?" he asked.

"Sunday."

"No, I mean the date."

"Um, October twelfth. No, thirteenth."

"We'll celebrate this as our anniversary."

Marcus kissed him. "Whatever you say."

"Just one thing," Bob said as he snuggled down into Marcus's lap and put his arms tightly around his waist. "If you ever cheat on me, I'll cut off your balls."

38

For the next ten days or so Marcus felt calm, content. He didn't think about the murder or much of anything, other than his classes, which were going well. On the Tuesday after their weekend he stopped at a jewelers in Harvard Square and bought two platinum rings. He tried his on and guessed that Bob's should be a size smaller. He would give it to him at Christmas.

Just as he got to his office, the phone rang. It was Deena. She had finally had a chance to read Marcus's pages, she said curtly, and summoned him to lunch the following day at the faculty club.

"Oh God," Marcus said out loud. He had put off deciding what to do about Deena, and her call brought it all crashing back.

That afternoon he had a department meeting, but he could hardly bring himself to listen. Two senior colleagues were arguing over a course requirement for the graduate program, and he really didn't care one way or the other. He thought about what Fred had said in New York, and he thought about Trip. One of his junior colleagues tried to make a point and was received with the usual withering glances from the senior faculty. This was one of those occasions when junior faculty were meant to be seen and not heard, like children at an adult's party. By now Marcus recognized the signs, knew when to keep his mouth shut. His young colleague did not.

He didn't sleep much that night, wondering how he would handle Deena's plagiarism. He supposed he should just go to the Dean and wash his hands of the whole matter.

Deena was not at all friendly when they greeted each other for lunch. She was wearing what women were coming to call a power suit, with a silk blouse and high heels. The dining room was crowded, and she stopped to talk to someone Marcus didn't recognize as they were shown to their table. He waited for quite a while for her to join him at the table. When she finally sat down she opened her menu and studied it. No small talk.

"Look," Deena said after they ordered. "I read your pages. And I have to say, I was disappointed." She then proceeded to tear his argument apart line by line.

Their food arrived, and Deena continued. Marcus didn't have to listen to the content of what she was saying; it was standard academic nitpicking. You repeat yourself here, your meaning is obscure there. You're echoing so-and-so on page four. Instead of listening to the content, he observed Deena's demeanor. It was haughty, there was no other word for it. Haughty and dismissive, cruel. Sadistic, even.

"I have to be frank, Marcus," she finally said. "This just isn't good enough for us. Honestly, if I were you, I'd start looking for another job. This is not the kind of original scholarship we expect."

Us.

We.

Years later, Marcus would realize that those were the

words that triggered him. He would learn over and over as time went by that life could turn on a tiny detail.

He had sent Deena roughly twenty pages, a short first draft, a brief excerpt from a what would someday be a book; it was not in any sense a finished product. And on the basis of a very small number of drafted pages, she was making a judgment about his worth as a scholar and his entire career. No room at the inn for you, young man. Leave now before we throw you out.

We.

Us.

Marcus took a sip of his iced tea. "I see."

Deena dug into her salad.

"So my analysis isn't as original as, say, your second book? I thought I was roughly in the same territory."

Deena suppressed a laugh. "Well, no, it isn't. Since you choose to put it that way."

A moment passed. Marcus put down his fork. "Tell me, Deena, when exactly did you discover the Dorothy Edgerly papers and proceed to make your original contribution?"

For a split second, Deena's face went red, but she quickly regained her composure. She put her own fork down, took a sip of water, and looked him squarely in the face. "If you have something to say, Marcus, please say it."

"All right." There was no turning back. "You plagiarized the argument of an unpublished scholar and made her material an integral part of your second book. That book helped you earn tenure. You are a fraud."

Deena smiled a half-smile. "And I suppose you discovered this through your snot-nosed student."

"As a matter of fact, I did. He had photocopies of material from the Edgerly papers. He saw the similarity right away. Not that it matters, but he didn't bring it to my attention while we were working together or while he was still a student. I found it by accident, going through some of the material left behind from his thesis. I recently went to Schlesinger and looked at the papers myself."

"You found it by accident?" Deena seemed incredulous.

"Yes. After his death"—Marcus emphasized the word—"the family asked me to look into things."

There was a long pause while Deena looked down at her plate. Marcus could feel sweat beginning to run down from his armpit.

Finally, Deena looked up and spoke. She kept her voice level, but Marcus could hear the tension underneath. "I will explain that some footnotes and quote marks were accidentally left out. I typed the manuscript on one of the new computers, using a complex word processing program for the first time. I had a research assistant, and she was as much at sea with the computer as I was. I'll issue a new edition and an apology. I'll say it was a mistake to use such a new device. That will be that."

"Do you really think people will accept that, Deena? You lifted whole paragraphs. Pages, even." Marcus couldn't tell if Deena had made up the story on the spot or had it ready.

"We're all new to computers. These footnote programs are complex. Perfectly understandable," she said smugly.

"We'll see."

"Marcus, if you accuse me of plagiarism, I will destroy you. You'll never get a job anywhere." She looked at him intently. Her face had hardened and seemed almost rigid.

"Have at it."

The lunch was over. This time it was Marcus who got up and left.

39

Out on the street, Marcus stood still for a moment, trying to return his breath and his heart rate to normal, with limited success. He had just accused a senior colleague of a serious offense, and maybe even implied that she could be guilty of murder.

Not what he'd expected to be doing here at the Center of Western Civilization, a phrase faculty and students applied to Harvard in jest. Mostly in jest.

Marcus started walking toward his office but decided to stop at the office of the dean of the faculty. He thought of an expression of his mother's: "In for a penny, in for a pound." And he remembered a quote attributed to Emerson, although he had never found the source: "When you strike at a king, you must kill him."

Only in this case, it was a queen.

University Hall stood at the center of Harvard Yard, with the famous statue of John Harvard in front of it. Students would sometimes rub the statue's toes on their way to exams. The inscription said "founder" under his name, but he wasn't actually the founder; he had donated books to the first library. Not to mention the person in the statue was probably not John Harvard. It was a landmark nonetheless.

Marcus walked into the dean's hushed outer office and approached one of the assistants. He identified himself and said he needed an appointment to see the dean as soon as possible.

"May I ask what this is in reference to?"

Marcus took a deep breath. "I have discovered incontrovertible proof of plagiarism on the part of a senior member of the faculty," he said, keeping his tone as steady as he could manage.

The assistant looked shocked but kept her cool. She rose and consulted another assistant, who consulted a third assistant, who came up to him.

"Professor George, can you return tomorrow morning at eight?"

"Yes, I'll be here. Thank you."

He went back to his office and sat at his desk for a long time, staring at the wall. He had a few appointments with students, so he couldn't leave. He called Bob at work and said he was taking him out to dinner at The Harvest.

"What's up?" Bob asked.

"A lot. I'll tell you when I see you."

He went to the men's room, used the facilities and stared at himself in the mirror while washing his hands. He couldn't decide if he was being careful or reckless, had no idea where any of this would lead, but knew he had started down a path and there was no getting off it now.

Back in his office, he dialed the Howard townhouse on Beacon Hill and spoke to Mrs. Howard. He said he had some information to share and asked if he could meet them the next evening. Mrs. Howard said yes, of course, and suggested he come at six. Then he then called Lieutenant Fitzgerald and asked if he could also be at the townhouse that day at six, without giving him too much detail. The lieutenant agreed.

Marcus carefully removed the photocopies of the Edgerly papers from the top drawer of his file cabinet. He took his own copy of Deena's book, marked the plagiarized passages in ink, and put the book and the photocopies in his briefcase.

He felt like he was on automatic pilot, in an altered state.

After his student appointments he went home, showered and changed. As he set out for The Harvest, fresh from his shower, he felt lighter. He would put both matters into the hands of the authorities, just as Fred Tucker had advised. The university would deal with the plagiarism, and the police, or the FBI, would deal with Deena as a suspect in Trip's murder. In twenty-four hours he'd be done, he told himself.

Years later, that sentiment made him laugh.

He greeted Bob at the restaurant with a long hug and they sat at a table near the bar. They ordered kir, white wine with crème de cassis, a cocktail that was all the rage for a few years on the East Coast and then disappeared completely.

"So is this where you tell me you have a wife and three children in Omaha?" Bob asked.

Marcus laughed. "No, this is where I tell you I'm done with Trip's case."

Bob listened avidly as Marcus narrated the day's events. "Wow!" he exclaimed.

They toasted. "To freedom," Marcus said.

Bob crinkled his forehead. "But can Deena really harm your career? It sounds like she meant it."

"Oh, she meant it. But soon she'll have no credibility at all, anywhere. It will be fine."

Bob nodded, but he wasn't convinced. Neither was Marcus.

They ordered dinner, leg of lamb. It was tender and subtly spiced, and they devoured it. Marcus realized he hadn't eaten much at the faculty club; Bob had had a yogurt for lunch at his desk.

After dinner they walked slowly home. It was chilly; the cold, wet, interminable Boston winter was definitely on its way, but there wasn't much wind that evening and it was still pleasant strolling outside. They bumped into a few of Marcus's undergraduates, two of whom stopped to chat. Marcus introduced Bob as his partner, the word gay men had started to use instead of "lover," which now sounded vaguely obscene as the epidemic was raging. Neither of them was entirely comfortable with the word "partner," which made them sound like they were in business together, but they didn't fight the trend.

At home they drank tea, ate some cookies that had just arrived from Danbury, and went to bed early. "I have to get mom's recipe for lamb," Bob mused, yawning.

Marcus slept better than he had for months.

40

Marcus arrived at University Hall a few minutes before eight. He was wearing his one good suit, dark gray, with a conservative tie. Bob had kissed him and wished him luck.

He took a seat in the dean's outer office and waited. And waited. Finally, after forty minutes, he was ushered into the inner office. It was huge, with a couch and chairs at one end, a large desk at the other, and a small conference table in the middle.

The dean, Miles Green, was an economist. It was a time when many universities were choosing economists as their leaders, presumably because investments had been so anemic in the 1970s. Green was respected and competent, everyone said. Marcus mostly ignored university-level politics. He didn't realize he was about to get a crash course.

After a moment Jack Steiner walked in; he was the campus counsel.

"I've asked Mr. Steiner to join us, given the nature of your allegation."

Marcus's nervous system went on high alert. Already his story was classified as an "allegation" and a lawyer was in the room. He tried not to focus on that single word as he told the story, telling himself to stay calm.

The two men listened carefully, their expressions neutral.

"Well, we will certainly look into the material you reference," the dean said.

"Actually, I have the proof here with me. May I show you? It won't take long."

The two men glanced at each other. They did not seem pleased. "Yes, if you'd like," Green said.

They moved to the conference table, and Marcus took the photocopies and the book out of his briefcase. Green and Steiner looked at the material as Marcus narrated, then looked at each other again, their expressions still neutral. They said nothing for a long moment. Finally, Green nodded to Marcus.

"I will certainly refer this to the appropriate university committee for consideration. Thank you for coming in," the dean said.

Marcus felt like he was getting what his father had called the bum's rush. He decided on the spur of the moment to press on.

"I'm afraid there's more. At this point, I'd say that Professor Echols has become a suspect in the murder of our recent graduate, Addison Howard, over the summer."

The dean and the lawyer both looked stunned. Neither moved. For a moment it seemed that Green had stopped breathing.

Marcus continued narrating, emphasizing that Trip had discovered the plagiarism and that the Howard family had asked him to look into the murder.

"Yes, I saw you lunching with him at the club," the dean said in a slightly less frosty tone. Finally, Marcus thought, something had pierced that cool, Ivy demeanor.

"Have you reported all this to the police?" Steiner asked.

"I will be doing so at a meeting this evening."

"You realize, of course, that that is an incredibly serious allegation."

"Yes. Of course."

There was an uncomfortable silence. By now it was after nine, and Green was running late. "I'm afraid we'll need to leave it there, I have to get on."

Green was from Rhode Island, Marcus knew. But he loved how Harvard faculty adopted British manners and phrases. He had a colleague, born in New Jersey, who pronounced "schedule" in the British way. "Get on" was pure British upper class.

They all stood. "Thank you, young man, for coming in."

And with that, Marcus was dismissed.

Young man. Something one would say to the grocery delivery boy.

41

Marcus had a sense of unease as he walked the short distance to his office, but he told himself the dean was just being discreet, businesslike. It was his first conversation ever with a university official at that level, and he didn't know how Green normally interacted. Maybe this was how he behaved with everyone. Reserved. Cards close to his chest.

Well, I just gave him a royal flush, Marcus thought to himself. *I hope he knows what to do with it.*

Marcus was busy for the rest of the morning. He had a class at eleven, then office hours and a committee meeting. In class they were approaching the Civil War and the debate about slavery, and for once the students seemed to have read the material and to be deeply engaged. That was what Marcus loved best, when he could get them interested, curious, excited. It didn't happen all that often, but when it did, it felt wonderful.

All day, he was mentally preparing himself for the meeting that evening with the Howards and Lieutenant Fitzgerald. Keep it simple and factual, he told himself.

Late in the day the phone in his office rang. It was Bob, who was off to interview a witness in his lawyer's current case in Dedham, a suburb of Boston south of the city, and probably wouldn't be home until fairly late. He wished Marcus luck with the Howards.

In the late afternoon Marcus went home, showered, changed, and then set off for Beacon Hill.

It was a chilly evening, the coldest so far that fall, and Marcus wore a wool pullover sweater and his overcoat. Winter was definitely on its way.

He arrived at the Charles Street station early and sauntered up and down the street for a bit, watching people on their way home from work. Beacon Hill in the 1980s was still a polyglot neighborhood, rich people, bohemians, artists, even some students sharing apartments. *It might be fun to live here*, Marcus thought. Just before six he made his way to Louisburg Square.

Trip's father (not the butler, Marcus noticed) opened the door and ushered him into the living room, where Fitzgerald, Trip's mother, and David Howard were seated on chairs and sofas. There was a fire in the fireplace, and subtle lights hidden in the ceiling had been turned on, along with some lamps. Everyone rose and shook Marcus's hand. Mrs. Howard offered him a drink, which he declined, and she pointed to a chair.

"Actually, it might be best if we sit around a table. I have some documents to show you."

They moved into the dining room. The housekeeper scurried to provide coasters for the drinks the others were carrying, and they arranged themselves around the no-doubt priceless antique table. Marcus sat and pulled Deena's book and the photocopies out of his briefcase.

"I've discovered something very disturbing," he began, "something that might advance the investigation into Trip's death."

Everyone looked startled. You could hear a pin drop, Marcus thought, except pins were undoubtedly the province of the servants downstairs.

He told the story as straightforwardly as he could: Trip's research, the Edgerly papers, the belated discovery of the plagiarism. He showed everyone the pages from Trip's photocopies, circled in red, and the pages in Deena's book. The group passed both around the table.

"Dorothy Edgerly was your cousin, is that correct, Mrs. Howard?"

She could hardly speak. "Yes. I told Trip about her." Tears formed in her eyes.

"From what I've gathered from what David said," Marcus continued, "Trip was vigilant about scandal, corruption."

David nodded.

"I know that Trip spoke to Professor Echols about his thesis; she's said as much. It's my belief that he confronted her with the plagiarism." He let their imaginations fill in the rest.

"Do you honestly believe this professor could have murdered Trip over this?" David seemed dumbfounded, as did his father. Fitzgerald looked skeptical.

"I don't know. I believe it's worth looking into. What I do know is that this level of plagiarism is a very serious offense, and will put Professor Echols's reputation, and maybe her position, in danger. Her career could come to a screeching halt."

Fitzgerald spoke up for the first time. "We'll certainly explore this."

David looked agitated. "Deena Echols is married to Jordan Echols, the attorney."

"Yes."

"He is a very high flyer in legal and political circles. The word is, he's on the short list for a judicial appointment," David said. He fidgeted and was getting more agitated by the minute.

"That may be," Fitzgerald said, "but we have to pursue this. And because the suspect lives in Massachusetts and the murder took place in Maine, I will have to inform the FBI."

There was a long silence.

"If only I hadn't told Trip about Dorothy," Mrs. Howard said, to no one in particular. She again had that faraway look in her eyes.

"You were trying to help," Mr. Howard said, and Marcus realized this was the first time he had seen him looking at his wife. "Thank you, Professor George, for bringing this forward," Howard said, and rose to signal that the meeting was over. Marcus had a sense of déjà vu; this felt a bit like the end of his meeting with the dean.

"I'll see you out," Mrs. Howard said.

"I'll be in touch," Fitzgerald told him as Marcus took his leave. Mr. Howard and David shook his hand.

The butler appeared out of nowhere to help him on with his coat. At the door, Mrs. Howard took his hand in both of hers, and said simply, "Thank you."

And with that, Marcus was outside. He looked back at the townhouse; the maid was drawing the curtains on the bowfront windows in the parlor, and he could see the three Howards standing there, backs toward the window, facing Lieutenant Fitzgerald.

He let out a deep breath and walked to the T station.

42

Marcus felt exhausted as he boarded the crowded car and rode to Cambridge, and even more exhausted as he exited at Harvard Square and walked through Harvard Yard to Kirkland St. The apartment was dark. Marcus fell onto the bed face down, not even pausing to take off his shoes. He dozed for ten minutes or so, then got up, washed his face, and ordered a large pizza, thinking Bob would want some when he got home. He knew anything with tomato sauce tasted better warmed up. That was one of the few things he knew about cooking.

The pizza arrived, and he ate three slices with a glass of red wine. Bob walked in, came straight into the kitchen, and sat down without taking off his coat.

"So?" he asked.

"So I told them. They seemed stunned."

"Well, that's natural. You'd just told them who might have murdered their son."

"Yes." Marcus got up and kissed Bob and helped him off with his coat. Bob grabbed a pizza slice, and Marcus poured him a glass of wine.

"So what happens now?" Bob asked.

Marcus thought for a moment. "They investigate." That

was the only thing Marcus was sure of at this point. "The FBI will have to be brought in, since it could involve interstate travel to commit a murder."

Bob let that sink in. "Oy."

"Oy indeed." Marcus let out a little laugh. "A lowly assistant professor has brought the FBI down on a senior colleague. Am I out of my mind?"

Bob frowned. "Marcus, what else could you do?"

"I guess."

"You had to tell them. Both the family and the police. You did your duty. If you hadn't, that could have been obstruction of justice."

"I suppose." Marcus tried to smile.

They polished off the pizza and the bottle of wine, and Bob said, "Let's go to Steve's for ice cream."

"It's forty degrees out there."

"So?"

"Pizza and ice cream. What would your mother say?"

"She'd say, 'How nice for you!' She takes her cues from Miss Manners."

Marcus laughed and got his coat.

At the ice cream shop they ran into a junior colleague of Marcus's and he waved, but she didn't wave back.

That's odd, Marcus thought. After he and Bob and shared a banana split, he said, "I'm going to go say hello to Julie." As he approached her table, smiling, Julie quickly put on her coat and signaled to her boyfriend that they were leaving. "Sorry, Marcus. I'm not interested in a scene."

He went back to his table, and Bob asked, "What was that?"

"That was the Harvard gossip mill in full gear. Fasten your seat belt."

43

They walked home and went straight to bed, and Marcus slept deeply. In the morning Bob had to leave early to interview another witness, so he was gone by the time Marcus got up.

Marcus made a cup of coffee and dialed Lieutenant Fitzgerald's number.

"That was quite a bombshell last night," was the lieutenant's greeting.

"Well, there's more. Some things I didn't want to talk about in front of the family."

"Go on."

Marcus told him what he had been able to learn about how Deena and Jordan Echols spent the Fourth of July, about the layout of the house and garage, about the people who were there and what they had said.

Fitzgerald listened and did not interrupt. He was clearly taking notes. He asked for identifying information about the guests at the Echols house on the Fourth.

"Very useful information. Thank you. We've already notified the FBI, and I'll be meeting with the special agent in charge this afternoon."

Marcus emphasized that he wasn't accusing anyone of

anything, only laying out the facts as he saw them, as the family had asked him to.

"They were shocked, no question. I think the brother was particularly shocked that a Harvard professor could be a serious murder suspect, given his ties to the place."

"Yes, I could tell. This was not what he expected to hear."

Over the next few days, Marcus did his best to get his life back to some semblance of normal. He taught his classes, graded papers, met with students. He swam at Blodgett Pool. Bob cheered him up, clearly relieved that Marcus had turned things over to the police, and Marcus noticed Bob seemed lighter, too, somehow. Marcus put the incident with Julie out of his mind.

A few days after his confrontation with Deena there was a knock on his office door, and Arthur Banfield asked if he was free for lunch. They arranged to meet at the Faculty Club.

When Marcus walked into the club lounge looking for Banfield, and then when they walked into the dining room, Marcus had the impression that people had been talking about him and that his appearance stopped their conversations. There were furtive glances followed by a quick turning away, a tight smile, an unmistakable change in the barometric pressure. One or two people nodded to their lunch companions as if to say, "That's the one." It wasn't terribly subtle.

Just keep walking, Marcus told himself, as they made their way toward their table at the back of the dining room.

He exchanged pleasantries with Banfield and they ordered. Then Banfield turned to him abruptly.

"What the hell were you thinking?"

"I beg your pardon?"

"What made you think you could do this?"

Marcus willed himself to stay calm. "Do what, exactly, Arthur?"

"Go after Deena Echols."

Marcus took a sip of his iced tea. "What should I have done, Arthur? I discovered blatant plagiarism. Should I have ignored it?"

"Your discovery, as you call it, apparently has made her a murder suspect. Do you have any idea what this scandal will do to us?"

That word again. Us.

"Arthur, Harvard has existed for three hundred and fifty years. I think it will survive."

Their food arrived, and they ate for a few minutes without saying anything.

"All right," Banfield said. "Tell me exactly how you discovered this alleged plagiarism."

Marcus told him about Trip's photocopies and Deena's book and going to the Schlesinger to examine the evidence himself. That Marcus had checked the original documents seemed to mollify Banfield somewhat.

"So what else could I do, Arthur, but go to the dean? What would you have done?"

"All right. I see what you're saying. But my boy, the storm that is going to come down on your head is not going to be pretty."

"What storm?"

Banfield lowered his voice. "Deena Echols is mobilizing her allies all over the campus, all over the country, in fact. She is saying the accusations against her are an attack on women in the academy."

"This has nothing to do with the fact that Deena is a woman."

"Yes, well, try telling that to Gwen over there." Banfield motioned toward Gwen Caserio a few tables away, the only woman tenured in the Physics Department, a legend among women in science.

Marcus was taken aback. This was an angle he had not considered. It was true Harvard had a woman problem; there were very few tenured women in any school of the university. There was in fact only one in his own large program. A university committee had recently been formed to look into the matter, one of those committees, everyone assumed, that would dutifully gather information and then write a report that would be quickly forgotten.

"Well, if Professor Caserio wants to look at the evidence, I'll be glad to show it to her."

They finished their meals. There were a few more furtive, awkward glances as they retrieved their coats and left the Faculty Club.

"Good luck, my boy. You're going to need it," Banfield said. And with that, he walked off toward the library.

Back in his office, Marcus reflected on what had just happened, what he'd just heard. He laughed to himself. Of course. Accuse a gay man of being a misogynist. How original. And how dangerous. For him. He steadied himself. Surely a University committee would vindicate his charge of plagiarism and that the storm would blow over.

But there was more, something else that bothered Marcus about the lunch even more than the charge of misogyny—Banfield's manner, the way he wanted to wash his hands of the whole story. Banfield was one of the few senior faculty members who paid any attention at all to Marcus, who occasionally invited him to lunch, took an interest, or pretended to take an interest, in his work. And he had walked off without expressing any condemnation of Deena's actions or any words of real support for Marcus, let alone any advice or offer of help.

"Good luck" was all Banfield had to offer. You're on your own, kid, see you around.

He turned back to the work on his desk but found it hard to concentrate. He read the same sentence in a student paper four times. He got up and started pacing.

"Goddamn it," he said out loud.

That evening he didn't tell Bob about the lunch, not wanting him to worry. And the next morning, when he woke to bright sunshine, he was determined to have a normal working day.

As he was getting ready to leave for the office, the doorbell rang. A man on the intercom said, "Special delivery." Marcus buzzed him in, opened the door, and was handed a thick, official-looking envelope, with the address of a law firm in the upper left corner. He opened the letter with a sinking feeling.

Deena was suing him for defamation.

44

Marcus had to get to his office; the graduate student writing on Thoreau would be there soon. As he walked he realized he wasn't entirely surprised by Deena's move. Her spouse was a hot-shot lawyer. And, as the saying went, the best defense was sometimes to go on offense.

The anxious graduate student was waiting on the bench next to Marcus's office door; Marcus brought him in, and they both settled into their chairs. Marcus tried to listen carefully but wasn't hearing much. He nodded here and there and hoped that would be sufficient as the student outlined his plan for his next chapter.

After he left, Marcus called Bob at his office. Bob worked for a lawyer and his father was a lawyer. One or both of them would know what to do about the defamation lawsuit. "We talk to Dad," Bob said. He knows enough people in Boston. He'll know who you should hire."

"Hire?"

"You need to hire a lawyer. You can't fight this by yourself." Marcus hadn't thought of that, but of course Bob was right.

That evening, after Bob's homemade lasagna, they called Danbury. Jake listened to Marcus's narration of the facts, asking just a few questions along the way.

"Her suit is total crap, of course, meant to distract. Meant to paint her as the victim. But it sounds like the plagiarism is clear. At an absolute minimum, you had reason to believe there was a serious problem in her book. Which means you had no choice as a professional scholar. Which means her suit has no merit."

Marcus felt greatly relieved.

"You'll win this fight, but, I'm sorry to say that your life may be misery for at least a few months because of it."

Marcus closed his eyes.

"I'll make a few calls. I'll find you the right attorney."

Marcus thanked him and handed the phone to Bob, who spoke to his father for a few minutes before he hung up and turned back to Marcus.

"Dad said don't worry about the cost of the lawyer. He'll cover it."

"What? That's incredibly generous, but I can't possibly let him do that."

"Yes you can. He's doing it for us. He said it's in lieu of a wedding present."

"Wedding present?"

"Yes. I've told them we're together now. Really together. For keeps."

"Bobby—"

"It's okay. Really."

Marcus was incredibly touched. He got up, went into the bedroom, and retrieved the two tiny boxes from the bottom drawer of his desk.

"Well, if we're official, let's make it really official," he said, handing Bob the smaller box.

Bob broke out into a huge smile, as he opened it. "Well.

It's not a diamond, but I love it. And you." He had tears in his eyes.

Marcus opened the other box, and they were both suddenly solemn as they put the rings on each other's fingers. Both fit perfectly.

"Oh, my. I'm a Sadie," Bob said, admiring the ring.

"Sadie?"

"Sadie, Sadie, married lady. That song. From *Funny Girl*. God, your education was incredibly incomplete. Are you sure you're gay?"

"Positive."

Marcus went into the living room and put on a record of big band music from the 1940s, then came back to the kitchen and pulled Bob to his feet.

They held each other close and danced until midnight.

45

In the morning Jake called with the names of two attorneys and said they were both excellent. Marcus thanked him but said he couldn't possibly accept his money.

"Don't be an idiot. Of course you can. You make slave wages. And you've made our son incredibly happy. Ruth said the moment she met you she knew you were a keeper."

"I do love him. If I could I would marry him."

"Someday. I'm sure."

Marcus called the first name Jake had given him, and was told the attorney was tied up in court for the next two weeks. When he called the second, Bill Schneider, he was put through immediately. They agreed to meet at five o'clock that afternoon.

Schneider's office was in one of the new towers on Boston's waterfront, all gleaming glass and steel. It was on the eighteenth floor and had a mesmerizing view of Boston Harbor. Everything was immaculate and spare.

A gorgeous female secretary showed Marcus in. Schneider shook his hand and introduced the other people in the room, an associate, and another secretary. Schneider was a well-tailored man of about fifty, with just a touch of what Marcus's grandmother would have called Jewish schlump. He led them all into an adjoining conference room. Schneider offered Marcus a drink and he asked for tea.

Okay," Schneider said, "start from the beginning and don't leave anything out, no matter how insignificant it seems."

Marcus took a breath. He started with Trip taking his classes and working on his thesis during his senior year, then the lunch in Cambridge in June, Miller's Cove, Bob, Lieutenant Fitzgerald, the Howards asking him to investigate. Both the secretary and the associate were writing everything down. Schneider listened.

"So this Maine lieutenant thinks that, without question, Ms. Echols is now a murder suspect?" he said when Marcus finished.

"Yes. Although how serious a suspect, I don't know."

"Well, there's one of your prime defenses right there. You had an obligation to come forward, inform the police. This is a nuisance lawsuit, meant to irritate you and put you on the defensive."

"Will we have to go to court?"

"I'd be surprised. In terms of the law, Echols is a public figure, or at least a limited public figure within academia and within Harvard. You showed no malice toward her, and you had a cordial relationship with her before this, correct?"

"I wouldn't say cordial. Collegial, perhaps."

"Okay, collegial. Now, let's look at those documents."

Marcus had brought the photocopies of the Edgerly papers and Deena's book. After examining them carefully, Schneider threw down his pen in disgust. "This lawsuit is the biggest bunch of crap I've seen in at least ten years, and that's saying something. This is a prima facie case of plagiarism."

Marcus relaxed and asked about next steps.

"I meet with her attorney, make it clear that if the suit goes forward, we'll go public with the evidence, and his client's reputation will be in tatters. They will drop the suit. Or rather, they should."

They discussed the financial arrangements. Marcus gulped at the hourly fee and signed a contract, wondering why he hadn't gone to law school.

He was told not to discuss the case with anyone, especially anyone at Harvard. The young associate walked him to the elevator and shook his hand. "We'll be in touch," he said.

As he made his way home, he thought to himself, *How the hell did I end up with a high-priced lawyer?*

46

Schneider called Marcus's office a few days later. "I'm afraid they're stonewalling. They want a court hearing, and it's been set for January."

"January?" Marcus was alarmed. Panicked, almost.

"January. Her lawyer said that Echols expects that Harvard will have cleared her of any wrongdoing by then. I can't imagine that will happen, so we just need to sit tight."

Marcus had a sinking feeling in his stomach. "What if we do go to court?"

There was a pause as Schneider said something to someone in his office. "You'd tell your story on the stand. We'd call Lieutenant Fitzgerald as a witness to show that Deena had become a murder suspect, as well as someone from the Howard family. We'd have to call someone from the Harvard administration. But believe me, it won't come to that. I will move to have the case dismissed before we ever get there."

Marcus felt reassured but still upset when he got off the phone. He told Bob about the conversation that night at dinner. Bob had said he'd be late that night, so Marcus had made his soy sauce chicken and a salad.

"This sounds like standard legal wrangling," Bob said,

biting into a chicken leg. "Let's drive down to Danbury this weekend and talk to Dad."

"Good idea. And I can thank them for the financial help."

The minute they arrived on Saturday, Bob showed Ruth his ring. "Look, Mom, I'm a Sadie!" Ruth laughed uproariously, kissed them both, and ushered them into the kitchen, where Jake was pouring wine.

"Wine with lunch, how decadent," Bob said, laughing.

They feasted on mushroom soup and sourdough bread and tuna casserole that was out-of-this-world delicious, and then poppy-seed cake and coffee. All three Abramsons were in a happy mood, and so was Marcus.

After lunch Bob said, "Dad, you need to reassure Marcus he isn't going to jail. Mom and I will clean up."

"Sure, sure," Jake said. "Can't have a son-in-law in jail."

Son-in-law? How on earth had this happened, Marcus wondered. An upper-middle-class Jewish family so completely comfortable with a gay son and his partner? The world tilted for Marcus, just a little. Despite AIDS, despite the complete indifference of the Reagan administration and thousands of gay men abandoned and dying, the world was tilting.

In the den Marcus told Jake what had transpired, what Schneider had said.

"I know it's hard to go through something like this, but he's right, the suit is total crap. I can't believe it won't get thrown out. Try not to worry. Schneider is great, and it sounds like he knows what he's doing."

It started snowing in the afternoon, and they all sat in front of the fireplace in the den, reading, talking, dozing. Marcus had brought a book on Melville. He gazed into the fire, at the snow falling. When he and Bob bought their dream home, he thought, it would have a fireplace. And a garden.

Ruth and Bob cooked dinner together, pot roast, gabbing away. They ate in the dining room. More wine, more giddy talk, more laughter. No wonder Bob had such a sunny personality.

Marcus and Jake did the dishes, and Marcus realized he felt more comfortable with Jake than he ever had with his own father. Then they all settled down to watch a film on television. Marcus had had so much wine and so much good food that he could hardly keep his eyes open; all he could remember was that the film had something to do with the Civil War. Ruth kept popping up to bring in cake and brownies from the kitchen. Marcus remembered something a friend had once said. For Catholics, salvation lies in the bedroom. For Protestants, at work. For Jews, in the kitchen.

On Sunday morning there were about four inches of snow on the ground under a bright sun. They had brunch—homemade French toast—then sat in front of another fire reading the Sunday papers until Marcus and Bob had to leave, with the usual care package tucked under Bob's arm.

"Remember," Jake said to Marcus. "Don't worry."

47

Marcus continued to notice curt glances and tight smiles from people on campus, but he told himself all that would pass when Deena was found guilty of plagiarism. He was still feeling the warm glow of Bob's family, the rings, what his life had become.

Then, a few days later, he received a letter via certified mail. The return address was Schneider's law firm. It stated that Mr. Schneider would not be able to represent him in the matter of the Echols lawsuit and advised him to seek counsel elsewhere. It did not give a reason.

Marcus felt like he had been run over by a truck. He walked around the Square in a daze, had dinner alone at a hamburger joint. Bob was away; his boss had sent him on an overnight to Albany to interview a witness.

Then, for good measure, things got worse. There was a knock on his office door the next day, and an undergraduate he had seen around came in. He introduced himself as Ralph Sedgwick, an editor at the *Crimson*. He was hoping to get a statement about the lawsuit filed against Marcus by Professor Deena Echols.

Marcus was silent, and Sedgwick seemed gratified by his discomfort. Finally Marcus said, "I'll have to think about whether I wish to say anything."

"The story is going to run tomorrow."

"In that case, I have no comment." Marcus stood and showed Sedgwick to the door. He immediately called Bob, told him what had happened, and said he needed to speak to Jake right away. Bob said he would locate him as fast as he could.

Marcus spent the next few hours in a daze, mostly sitting at his desk and staring out the window. It was sleeting.

By five there was no call from Bob or Jake, and Marcus walked home. An hour later the phone rang.

"It was pressure from Jordan Echols, the husband, and his firm," Jake said.

"Oh. I guess I shouldn't be surprised."

"Schneider's firm and Echols have some interests in common, some case they were working on, probably. It's possible they thought there was conflict of interest. I wasn't able to find out the details. I'm sorry, terribly sorry. But don't worry, I got you into this mess, and I'll get you out. I'll find you someone else."

Marcus told Jake about the *Crimson* reporter. Jake agreed he should say nothing, at least for the moment.

Marcus got off the phone and called Gary Williams. Their therapy sessions had been irregular, what with Marcus's schedule and Gary's.

"I need to see you as soon as possible."

48

Bob came home and did his best to cheer Marcus up, but Marcus could tell he was worried too. And Bob was a bit ticked off at his father, though obviously, as they both said, there was no way Jake could have foreseen what happened with Schneider.

In the morning, Marcus stopped on campus to pick up a copy of the *Crimson* on his way to see Gary. There was a long front-page story with a headline in large type, in which Deena all but accused Marcus, by name, of crimes against humanity. She called him "petty" and "vindictive" and "someone who apparently has problems with women in positions of authority." And she said that the "so-called" plagiarism was due to problems with a new computer and its footnote program. Her statements about him were so over the top that his terse "no comment" sounded statesmanlike in comparison. Or so he hoped.

The most alarming thing in the article, however, was the last paragraph. "The *Crimson* attempted to compare Professor Echols's work to the original Edgerly papers, but that collection has been removed from the Schlesinger Library. The staff of the library could not be reached for comment."

When he read that, Marcus felt almost physically dizzy.

He made his way to the T and Gary's house in Brookline.

"I think I'm in trouble," he said before either of them had a chance to sit down.

"How so?"

Marcus filled him in on what had been happening.

"I'm sure this isn't pleasant, but if you're confident that you did the right thing, you just have to continue doing what you're doing, as calmly as possible."

It was the kind of thing Gary said, as if you could make up your mind to stay calm and that was that. *Clearly*, Marcus thought, not for the first time, *Gary's not Jewish*.

"Everything is in the mind," Gary continued. "All this upset. Your mind is doing this to you." Gary often repeated that phrase, and it always struck Marcus as ridiculous.

"That newspaper story this morning, and a lawsuit against me, and a lawyer dropping me, those aren't in my mind."

"No. But you can choose how to react to them." Round and round they went.

Back on the T after the session, Marcus wondered if there was anything he could do to counter the *Crimson* article, but he realized he needed a lawyer's advice about what to do or say—or not do or say. The one thing that might help turn the tide, he thought, would be if Deena were publicly identified as a suspect in Trip's murder.

Marcus taught his eleven o'clock class, then went home; he was not going to have lunch at the Faculty Club or anywhere in the Square, at least not today. He ate peanut butter and jelly and drank some scotch and considered what to do next.

A copy of *The Boston Globe* lay on the table, and he

remembered Simmons, the reporter who had broken the story on Frank Murphy and had interviewed David Howard about corruption on the Boston City Council. He dialed Simmons's number, asked if they could meet.

Late that afternoon they met at the same Boston pub as before. Marcus thanked him for coming and said that every part of their conversation would have to be completely off the record. Simmons agreed.

Marcus showed him the *Crimson* article and told him what was happening, and Simmons took notes. Marcus emphasized that the Miller's Cove police now considered Deena a murder suspect, and that there were no other suspects at the moment, as far as he knew.

Simmons was noncommittal but said he would talk to his editor and do some additional research. He thanked Marcus and left.

In for a penny, in for a pound, Marcus thought. He finished his seltzer and went home.

The article appeared in the *Globe* a few days later. It identified Deena as a Harvard professor under investigation for alleged plagiarism and identified her as a "person of interest" in the Miller's Cove investigation of Trip's murder.

The *Crimson* reported the murder story the next day.

Marcus taught his classes, held his office hours, and ate lunch at his desk. The glares and slights from others on campus intensified. A few times, walking to his office or to the library, he got the distinct impression that people were changing their route to avoid bumping into him.

He thought again about the meaning of the word "pariah."

The day after the *Globe* story, Jake Abramson called with the name of a new attorney, Lisa Rosenthal, and Marcus made an appointment with her for the next evening.

Her office was in an older building in a slightly shabby section of downtown Boston, but the office itself had been renovated and was bright and cheerful. Rosenthal herself greeted Marcus in the reception area. She was a strikingly attractive woman in her early thirties, he guessed, with auburn hair and blue eyes. Her firm was considerably smaller than Schneider's.

"Thank you for seeing me so quickly, Ms. Rosenthal," Marcus said.

"Please, it's Lisa, and it's my pleasure. I'm intrigued by your case."

She showed Marcus into her office, where two other attorneys and a secretary were waiting. He could see copies of the *Globe* and *Crimson* articles on the conference table. He noticed diplomas on the wall; Rosenthal had gotten her law degree at Yale.

Thank God, he thought.

Marcus narrated the story as he had for Schneider and showed them the evidence, the Edgerly photocopies and the passages from Deena's book. The secretary went out to make copies of the copies and the pages from the book.

"Okay," Lisa said. "I meet with her attorneys and demand that they drop the suit. The longer this drags on, the more identified Echols becomes with plagiarism. Not good for her. That may work. It may not. If it doesn't, we present the evidence at the court hearing in January. We make clear that Echols is a murder suspect, and we argue that this is a frivolous lawsuit meant to distract. Worst-case scenario, the defamation suit goes to trial, and you win. This isn't defamation, its responsible academic citizenship."

Marcus was impressed; he felt like he was in capable

hands. He mentioned the awkwardness for him on campus and asked if it would make sense to put out the evidence of plagiarism sooner rather than later. Lisa thought for a moment, glanced at her colleagues.

"Let's hold off. I may need that as a bargaining chip. It gives us leverage. Do you know how long the internal review will take at Harvard?"

Marcus said he had no idea.

"I'm afraid you'll need to tough things out on campus, at least for a little while. I know it won't be pleasant, or easy. But it could pay off."

Marcus nodded.

When he got home that night, he recounted the day's events to Bob.

"Smart of Dad to choose a female attorney this time," Bob said, and Marcus had to agree. He hated the gender politics of what was happening, but decided if Deena was going to play that card, he needed every advantage he could get.

"Mom called. She wants us to come down for Thanksgiving."

Marcus had almost forgotten that the holidays were fast approaching. "Yes, sure. It will be good to get the hell out of Dodge."

"Don't get any crazy ideas about shooting up the bad guys, Marshal Dillon," Bob said, batting his eyelashes. "Miss Kitty needs you."

49

Marcus did his best over the next week to focus on his work and not obsess about the lawsuit, or about anything else. One afternoon, the phone in his office rang, and he was surprised to hear Mrs. Howard's voice on the other end of the line. She invited him to tea the next day in Louisburg Square.

It was now mid-November, and the weather was dreadful as Marcus made his way to Beacon Hill. Mrs. Howard herself opened the townhouse door and ushered him into the front parlor, where a fire had been lit. The butler took his coat. Mrs. Howard was wearing a long gray skirt, a silk blouse, and perfectly matched pearls.

As they settled in two chairs near the fireplace, the butler poured Marcus a cup of tea and offered a slice of cake, which he declined.

Mrs. Howard sipped her tea. "We've seen the stories in the press, we know you're being sued. We're so very sorry. How are you coping?"

Marcus said he was doing his best to concentrate on his work, that he had a good lawyer who was confident he would win, one way or another.

"Yes, Lisa Rosenthal. She seems like a very good choice."

Marcus wondered how she could possibly know that Lisa was his new attorney. Before he could organize his thoughts about that, Mrs. Howard said that her husband had made it clear to Harvard officials that they had indeed asked Marcus to look into Trip's death and that they appreciated his efforts.

Marcus was getting a crash course in how the world of the elites actually worked. "Thank you for telling me that, and please thank your husband. Things have been less than easy for me in campus."

"I can imagine."

Mrs. Howard turned the talk to the upcoming holidays, and Marcus mentioned the Christmas caroling he had seen on the square in the past.

"Yes, that still goes on," Mrs. Howard said with a smile. "We're usually up in Maine, though, so most years we've missed it."

They chatted for a while longer, and Marcus asked about the painting above the fireplace. "Is that Kandinsky?"

Mrs. Howard smiled. "Yes. You have a good eye. A wedding present from my parents."

Marcus wondered what it would be like to be brought up in a family where such things were given as gifts.

As if reading his thoughts, Mrs. Howard said something that struck Marcus as quite odd. "It's not all roses, this kind of life, you know. It has its ups and downs."

"I'm sure. Every life does." Marcus didn't know what else to say, but he knew he would have traded uptown Chicago for this in a minute.

It wouldn't be long before he revised that judgment.

50

A few days later, Lisa Rosenthal called. "Bad news, I'm afraid. They won't drop the suit."

"Did they say why?" It felt like another body blow, but by now Marcus was getting used to them, at least a little.

"Not in so many words. They seem to think Echols will be vindicated on the plagiarism."

"I see," was all Marcus could bring himself to say. He gathered his thoughts. "But even if she is vindicated—even if Harvard accepts her story—it doesn't necessarily follow that she was defamed."

"Exactly. We'll prevail at the hearing. Try not to worry. Have a good holiday. Try to forget all of this."

"By the way, have you had any contact with the Howard family?" Marcus asked. "Just curious."

There was a long pause. "I knew David Howard at Boston Latin." Boston Latin was a prominent local prep school. "In fact, we dated for a while, but I don't think his parents approved."

"Oh?"

"My last name. The father objected, I think. I don't think his mother did. I think she quite liked me."

"The Howards know you're my attorney. Any idea how?"

Lisa thought for a moment. "Well, I've been in touch with the Echols attorneys, of course. A couple of the partners there know David and Trip's father, and must have told him."

"I see. Small world."

"In fact," Lisa went on, "the Howards had their personal attorney contact me and offer to pay your legal expenses."

Marcus was stunned yet again. "I see." That was how these people operate. They didn't tell you, they just did things.

He tried to remember what life was like just six months ago, before he got tangled up with the very rich.

51

Marcus taught his last class before Thanksgiving on Tuesday, and drove to Danbury with Bob on Wednesday morning. The roads were jammed, and there was snow as they left Boston, which turned to sleet and then hard rain as they drove south.

"New England weather," Bob said. "Gotta love it."

"That's one good thing about winter in Chicago," Marcus said. "By this time of the year, if it's going to do anything, it's going to snow. None of this temperature hovering around thirty-two degrees. It's colder, but it's a dry cold."

Bob laughed. "Dry cold. That's a good one."

Ruth greeted them warmly, as always. They arrived in time for a late lunch, tomato soup and tuna sandwiches. Food was spread out everywhere in the kitchen in various stages of preparation. The dining room table was already set for eight, with china, silverware, flowers.

After lunch Ruth sent them out to the grocery store and the liquor store with a list. By the time they got back, Jake was home, and everyone was put to work chopping, dicing, slicing. Ruth and Jake and Bob gabbed away; it all felt to Marcus like something out of Norman Rockwell.

For dinner they ordered pizza, which came late—

everyone in Danbury apparently had the same idea that night—and Bob made a salad. They drank copious amounts of red wine.

"So, how's the case going?" Jake asked.

Marcus took a sip of wine. "We're on pause." He filled them in with the details and again expressed his gratitude for their financial help. He promised to pay them back.

"Don't worry about that," Jake said. "You have enough to think about. Being involved in a lawsuit, having to defend yourself, it's horrible. Believe me, I know, but I just can't believe the suit will go very far."

Marcus smiled. "As my mother used to say, from your mouth to God's ears."

"Tell us about your family," Ruth said.

"Not much to tell, really. My father grew up in LA, came to Chicago for college, met my mother. They married in 1939, just before the war, both very young. My mother was eighteen. When my father got out of the army they ran a store that had belonged to my mother's father, selling household goods, wallpaper, paint, that sort of thing."

"Any siblings?"

"A brother and a sister, both older, both married."

"Are you close?"

"I'm in touch with my brother and sister, but to be honest, I'm not close to my mother. My father died a few years ago. They both had trouble with the idea of a gay son, my mother more so."

"A lot of people of their generation find it hard, I imagine," Ruth said, and Marcus realized that she and Jake were at least ten years younger than his parents.

Ruth seemed to sense that Marcus didn't want to say more about his family, so she changed the subject to the schedule for the next day. Guests were coming around five, dinner would be at six. She ran through the list of things that had to be done in the morning, which was formidable.

Upstairs, Bob said he hoped his mother's questions hadn't upset Marcus.

"No, no, not at all. It's natural that she'd be curious." They tried to have sex in one of the narrow twin beds and ended up on the floor, laughing hysterically.

The morning was a flurry of cooking, and soon enough the guests arrived, two sets of youngish cousins, all happy to meet Marcus, all friendly and warm. Dinner was spectacular, a perfect turkey with all the trimmings and then some, and the conversation and wine flowed. After dinner Jake brought out a bottle of very old brandy, and Marcus had never tasted anything quite like it.

On Friday, they all lounged around. Marcus read a book on the abolitionists in front of the fire. Friday evening they went to a local diner for dinner, and everyone there seemed to know the Abramsons. One young woman who'd gone to high school with Bob came over and gave him a hug. He introduced Marcus to her as his partner, and there was that familiar split-second adjustment, when someone realizes for the first time that a friend or relative really is gay. Marcus knew that look well.

They left Saturday morning after hugs all around. Marcus drove, and as they hit the outskirts of Boston, sped past the usual exit. Bob looked at him. "Where are we going?"

"The beach."

"You realize it will be freezing there, and the town may be empty?"

"Oh, come on, where's your sense of adventure? Aren't you one of those hardy New Englanders?"

"Hardy? Hardly. We're sissies, remember?"

The town wasn't empty at all, and they found their inn on the hill was open and had a room available. The innkeeper and his boyfriend seemed happy to see them. The innkeeper noticed their matching rings and beamed at them.

"Ah, l'amour, l'amour" he said dreamily. Bob had to explain that that was a famous line from *The Women*, uttered by a much-married countess in between husbands.

They settled in and then walked down the hill to Maineium's for a late lunch. It was indeed a very cold day, with the wind coming off the ocean. They sat in one of the red leather booths and ordered chili and hot tea.

Marcus looked around.

"You're hoping that lieutenant walks in so you can ask him about the case, aren't you?" Bob asked.

Marcus pretended to be shocked. "Lord, you have a suspicious mind. Can't a guy do something spontaneous once in a while?"

"Looking around a diner like you're looking for a long-lost lover is spontaneous? Don't try to fool me."

Marcus burst out laughing.

Fitzgerald didn't come in for lunch, so Marcus called him from the inn and was told he was off for the weekend. They bundled up as much as they could and took a long walk on the beach, then a nap, then went to their Italian restaurant for dinner.

"I love this place," Marcus said, looking out at the street.

52

On Monday morning, bright and early, there was a knock on Marcus's office door, and Rachel Hoffman, the one tenured woman in his program, walked in. She had the most brilliant mind he had ever come across, Marcus thought, and had always been cordial to him. Born Jewish in Berlin, she escaped with her family when the Nazis came to power and had had a brilliant career in the U.S. as a cultural theorist and critic, with a special interest in the language of diplomacy. It was said that one of her books was required reading for serious diplomats everywhere.

"All right," she said, wasting no time, as usual, "what have you gotten yourself into?"

Marcus told her about discovering the plagiarism and showed her the photocopies and the passages in Deena's book. She looked them over.

"Deena says the problem was the footnote program on these damn new computers. Is that so hard to believe?"

"Rachel, she reprinted whole paragraphs. Edgerly is not mentioned anywhere—not in footnotes, not in the text, not in the acknowledgments. Does that strike you as an accident?"

"I don't know," Rachel said, pushing the photocopies away. "What I do know is that you have made a powerful enemy. Do what you can to settle this damned lawsuit. It's terrible for us."

That word again, Marcus thought to himself.

With that, Rachel took her leave.

Later in the day, Marcus received a phone call from the dean's office to schedule his time before the faculty committee that had been charged with reaching a judgment about the allegation of plagiarism against Deena Echols. The date was in two weeks, in mid-December. He asked if he was allowed to have counsel present, and the assistant to whom he was speaking was taken aback. She said she'd have to check and get back to him.

Marcus taught his eleven o'clock class and then ate a yogurt at his desk. Just before his afternoon office hours began, he called Lieutenant Fitzgerald and asked him what was happening in the investigation of Deena as a suspect.

"I shouldn't really talk about the case at this point."

"Lieutenant, I'm in serious trouble at Harvard for having pursued this matter and bringing Deena Echols to your attention. I don't think it's asking too much for an update. It can be completely off the record."

There was a long pause.

"Please," Marcus added.

"All right. But do not share this information with anyone, not even with anyone with whom you may be intimate."

Couldn't bring himself to say boyfriend or partner, Marcus thought. *So much for progress.*

"The case has been taken over by the FBI. Deena Echols has what they say is a credible alibi concerning her whereabouts on the Fourth."

"Their party?" Marcus was dubious. "The party where she excused herself and went upstairs?"

"Her husband has testified that he went upstairs to check on her several times, and one of the other guests corroborates that she was there. They bumped into each other when the guest was looking for a bathroom. The husband is a very well-connected attorney. He knows what it could mean if he lied to the FBI."

There was another long pause.

"She didn't do it," Fitzgerald said. I know this may complicate your professional life, but obviously that can't influence the investigation."

"No, of course not." Marcus didn't know what else to say. After a moment he asked, "Are there any other suspects?"

"Not at this time. But the investigation is still open and the FBI is actively pursuing it. There has been considerable pressure to continue the investigation from the Howard family. They are extremely well connected, not just around here but in Washington."

"Yes, I'm sure they are," Marcus said with a wry chuckle. He thanked Fitzgerald for the information.

The rest of the afternoon was a blur. Marcus met with some students and did some paperwork, and then walked home on a cold, windy afternoon.

The person with whom he was intimate came home and kissed Marcus on the cheek while taking off his coat. They moved into the kitchen, where Bob began whipping up some kind of casserole while Marcus recounted the day to him and made a salad.

"Well, if Deena didn't kill Trip, who did?" Bob asked.

"Apparently they have no idea."

Bob could tell Marcus was upset. He stopped stirring and took Marcus by the shoulders. "Listen to me. She may not be a murderer, but that doesn't change what you found out about her book. You did the right thing."

"Did I? I don't know anymore." In truth, everything seemed like such a mess that Marcus felt like he no longer knew anything about anything.

"Marcus. Listen to me. You go to the hearing. You tell them what happened. End of story."

Marcus tried to smile. "Yes, sir."

53

The semester was drawing to a close, which meant that Marcus was busier than usual on campus, more panicked students in his office, longer office hours. He met with Lisa Rosenthal to prepare for his appearance before the plagiarism committee; he had been told that he could not bring an attorney with him to the hearing. "You are a witness, not the accused," a Dean's assistant had said to him sternly.

Lisa advised him to tell the truth, to answer only the questions he was asked, and not to embellish or provide commentary or opinion unless absolutely necessary. Marcus nodded, but he knew it would be hard not to offer an opinion.

The day of the hearing arrived; his appearance was scheduled for 9:00 a.m. Marcus wore his good suit and Bob picked out his tie—orange and black, Princeton's colors.

"Always fly the Ivy flag," Bob said.

Marcus laughed. "Then shouldn't I wear crimson?"

"No," Bob said. "Ivy yes. Harvard lapdog, no."

Marcus made his way to campus on that cold, sunny morning and sat outside a conference room in University Hall until was brought before the committee a few minutes after nine.

Seated around the long oval conference table were five

distinguished-looking faculty members, all men, all white, all wearing what seemed like matching dark suits. Marcus recognized only one, Arthur Spence, an economist and Nobel laureate. The others were not introduced; in typical Harvard fashion, he was simply supposed to know who they were. He was offered coffee, which he accepted as he took his seat at the foot of the table.

Spence asked him to relate the facts that led him to his accusation of plagiarism, and Marcus did so, telling the story for what by now felt like the hundredth time. A stenographer in one corner recorded his testimony.

One of the committee members then asked a series of questions. "You visited the dean's office to report this matter after a lunch with Professor Echols, is that correct?"

"Yes."

"Please tell us what transpired at that lunch."

"Professor Echols gave me feedback about some work I had shown her, a few pages from the draft of a book chapter."

"Is it fair to say the feedback was negative?"

"Yes."

"And then you immediately accused Professor Echols of plagiarism, did you not? Does that not suggest you were simply angry at Professor Echols's feedback?"

Marcus took a sip of his coffee. He'd expected this question and had rehearsed an answer with Lisa Rosenthal.

"I thought Professor Echols displayed extraordinary arrogance in the manner in which she responded to my work. It was just a few pages, a very short draft. On the basis of that, she advised me to leave Harvard and seek employment elsewhere."

He paused for a moment to let that sink in.

"Plagiarism also involves extraordinary arrogance. Since Professor Echols herself was tenured here in part on the basis of work that was, in my opinion, blatantly plagiarized from another source, I thought her response to my own work was similarly unprofessional."

"Be that as it may, why did you immediately report to the dean?"

"Because when confronted, Professor Echols said, in so many words, that she would offer an excuse for the plagiarism, and then she threatened me. Threatened me in the extreme."

"You call it an excuse. Why not call it an explanation?"

"Because both in content and in form it sounded like an excuse."

"You say Professor Echols threatened you. Were you not the one threatening her?"

"I don't say 'she threatened me' lightly, sir. She told me she would destroy my career. If that is not a threat, by a tenured professor to someone younger and untenured, I don't know what you would call it. Furthermore, if the plagiarism in question, which led to the threat, was inadvertent or a mistake, as Professor Echols now claims, why had the error not been acknowledged and corrected already?"

Before his questioner could continue, Marcus cut him off.

"Gentlemen, Professor Echols displayed extreme and unprofessional arrogance. First, blatantly stealing the work of another scholar, and then dismissing the work of yet another scholar, myself. No regard for the work or reputation of either of us. Dorothy Edgerly and I deserved ordinary professional courtesy: at a minimum, acknowledgment and citation in the case of Dr. Edgerly, and with me, the benefit of the doubt that those few pages would be revised and were not going to be the sum total of a much longer monograph in progress. Neither one of us received that professional courtesy from Professor Echols. Obviously, the plagiarism is far the more serious of the two matters."

Marcus could tell that his words had an impact on at least one or two committee members. There was a pause. He was asked a few more perfunctory questions and then was thanked for his time.

Dismissed.

He had just a few minutes to collect himself and get to his class.

When Marcus entered the classroom in his suit and tie, the students in unison said "ahhh."

"Yes, it's true. I own a suit. The Crimson Shop's finest." Marcus opened the suit jacket to show the silk lining.

One of the students in the back said, "That's a Princeton tie," and everyone gave a disapproving "ohhhh."

Marcus laughed and removed the offending tie. They clapped.

"Now, if you could turn your attention away from my wardrobe, we need to discuss the political rhetoric of the New Deal."

Somehow he got through the class and then had arranged to meet Bob for lunch at The Harvest.

"The Harvest?" Bob had been surprised the night before.

"The Harvest. Someplace with alcohol."

54

He arrived before Bob and ordered a scotch. He almost never drank hard liquor, and never with lunch, but then he had never been through anything like that hearing.

When Bob joined him, Marcus recounted the morning. He was feeling lightheaded and a little giddy. Bob told him it sounded like he said exactly what needed to be said.

"Bobby, I love you. Let's go home and take off all our clothes."

"You are a dirty old man and tipsy. I am going back to work."

Marcus suddenly realized, with horror, that he had a search committee meeting that afternoon and should not have had anything to drink. Outside the restaurant he hugged Bob and rushed back to campus.

At the meeting a decision needed to be made about hiring a new assistant professor to teach the literature and culture of the Soviet Union. Marcus had been added to the committee as the obligatory junior member, and though it was a field he knew very little about, he was a good citizen and went to all the committee meetings and job talks, most of which were dreary beyond belief.

Today the rest of the search committee was recommending

a candidate with a Stanford PhD whose dissertation was on the Russian penchant for authoritarian leaders, starting with Lenin. The dissertation was highly quantitative, counting the number of references to certain terms and phrases in the speeches of Lenin and the leaders who came after him.

After listening to his senior colleagues debate the candidate's merits, Marcus spoke.

"How is it possible to talk about the Russian attachment to authoritarian leadership without talking about the czars? How is it possible to talk about Lenin as a cult figure without talking about Nicholas and the royal family?"

Marcus hated the ahistoricism that seemed to be sweeping so many disciplines.

Everyone stared at him, and Marcus realized that the scotch he had drunk at lunch had had its effect; junior faculty were supposed to be seen and not heard at these meetings.

For a moment, no one said anything. Then Sam Cochran cleared his throat. "Perhaps Marcus makes a good point."

The discussion continued, but in a changed direction, and the consensus seemed to be to extend the search, go back into the pool and see if there was anyone else who could be brought in for an interview. The Stanford candidate would be held in reserve.

Marcus had scuttled the search committee's work, at least for the time being. He felt sheepish, but when one of the senior members glared at him as the meeting broke up, he found himself glaring back.

Speaking out, he suddenly realized—as he had with Deena, as he had with the plagiarism committee, as he had just now— was the way he wanted to conduct himself as an academic.

"So be it," he said aloud when he got back to his office.

55

Classes ended with the usual rush of business, and then it was Christmas. Marcus and Bob decided to spend four or five days in Danbury and another four or five in Miller's Cove, where their inn was open for the holidays and then closed until late April.

"We celebrate Jewish Christmas," Bob told Marcus.

"I beg your pardon. What is that?"

"A movie and Chinese food."

Marcus laughed. "So when do you exchange gifts?"

"The day after Christmas. Don't ask me why. No one knows."

They couldn't decide what to buy Bob's parents, and finally settled on making a contribution to the ACLU in their honor, along with a book on tennis for Ruth and a book on the history of civil rights for Jake. Marcus bought Bob a watch, which he needed, and Bob bought Marcus a new briefcase with engraved initials. They told Bob's parents not to get them anything since they were already paying Lisa Rosenthal, but Ruth and Jake got them matching sweaters anyway. They exchanged all the gifts the day after Christmas just as Bob had said they would. On Christmas Eve they had gone to see *Desperately Seeking Susan*, which they all enjoyed, especially Ruth, who couldn't stop laughing.

A few days later Marcus and Bob drove to their inn. There was only a sprinkling of other guests, and the town was more shut down than it had been at Thanksgiving, but several of their favorite places were open, including Maineium's. They walked around town and on the beach, stopping to talk to a few of the locals and wish them a happy new year. Everyone seemed to be in a carefree mood despite the cold and the howling wind off the ocean.

Among the guests at the inn was a gay couple from Portland: Bill, who was on the staff of Portland's mayor, and Doug, a lawyer. The four of them had a jolly dinner together at the Italian place on New Year's Eve, drinking late into the evening. The waiters all wore funny hats and passed out noisemakers.

On New Year's Day they drove back to Cambridge and collected their accumulated mail. Marcus opened a plain envelope with no return address containing a single sheet of paper labeled "Press Release, Women's Caucus of the Modern Language Association." He sat down at his desk to read it while Bob went to the grocery store. He knew it would not be good news.

Deena Echols had been elected chair of the Caucus, which was issuing this statement "of unanimous support," urging Harvard to exonerate her of "the baseless charge of plagiarism that has been leveled against her."

Marcus had reached the point where nothing that happened in the whole mess surprised him. He threw the press release away.

On January 3, he began meeting with Lisa Rosenthal to discuss the upcoming court hearing on the lawsuit against him. Lisa carefully walked him through what would happen, and together they rehearsed his testimony. One of Lisa's associates played the role of Deena's attorney and did a very good job. Marcus was flustered by his questions.

"Keep your demeanor cool," Lisa said. "That is incredibly important. Pause if you need to. Straighten your tie, take out a handkerchief and blow your nose. Whatever it takes to buy a little time and compose yourself."

She went on to explain that the hearing was in response to her formal motion to dismiss the case. It was akin to a probable cause hearing in a criminal matter, to see if there was sufficient reason for moving forward. Their argument was straightforward: Marcus had discovered a professional problem and reported it to the appropriate authorities. He had no alternative but to do so. The plagiarism in question was, in his professional opinion, clear cut, and he had no way of investigating whether it was intentional or some kind of mistake, although the amount of material copied was, in fact, massive.

The hearing day arrived, January 14. The temperature was three below zero, the wind was punishing, and everyone in the courtroom was shivering. Deena strode in with not one, not two, but three attorneys at her side. Her husband sat in the near-empty gallery. Bob had taken the day off to be there and sat on the opposite side of the courtroom, along with someone Marcus did not recognize. He knew that Lieutenant Fitzgerald and an FBI agent were waiting in separate witness rooms; standard procedure, Lisa had said, to keep witnesses apart so they couldn't collude.

The judge entered, told everyone to be seated, and turned to Marcus's side of the courtroom. "Ms. Rosenthal, please begin."

Lisa rose and began laying out their case. Almost

immediately, one of Deena's attorneys objected, and the two of them began arguing. The judge called them to the bench.

They were sent back to their places and the judge told Lisa to continue her statement. As she was finishing, she asked that "certain documents" be placed in evidence, namely the photocopies of the Edgerly papers and a copy of Deena's book. All three of Deena's attorneys rose to their feet in unison and said, "Objection!"

The judge could not get them to stop objecting, and finally banged his gavel. "I will see counsel in chambers," he said sternly.

They were gone a long time. Finally, Lisa returned to the table.

"What's happening," Marcus asked.

Lisa smiled. "The judge is going to recess the hearing to examine the material. That's what we needed to happen."

The judge returned and recessed the hearing for two hours.

Lisa, Marcus, and Bob walked over to a coffee shop across the street from the courthouse. No one said much of anything. Marcus was drumming his leg under the table and Bob put his hand on his knee to stop him. They drank coffee and waited.

"Nothing's more tiring than waiting for something," Bob said.

When they got back to the courtroom, the judge gaveled court into session and then once again said he would see counsel in chambers.

They were gone a long time, and despite the cold, Marcus was sweating. When they returned, Lisa was smiling. The judge gaveled the court into session.

"The case is dismissed," he announced. And banged his gavel.

Just like that.

Deena and her retinue glared at them and stormed out.

Marcus sat back down. "What just happened?" he asked. Bob came up and sat just behind the railing and put his hand on Marcus's shoulder. They turned to Lisa.

"Well. First, the judge said that the lawsuit was frivolous. He said there was a prima facie case of plagiarism involved, and reporting it to the Harvard authorities could not therefore be defamatory, whatever the final disposition of the case."

"So we won on the merits?" Marcus asked.

"Yes. At least with this judge. Her lawyers objected strenuously, and said they would appeal the ruling. Then I said that if the suit went forward, we would make it clear that what you found in those papers was enough to make Echols a suspect in a case of first-degree murder. That's why I made sure the Maine police and the FBI were ready to testify and that a reporter from the *Globe* was in the courtroom today." Lisa gestured toward the spot where the unidentified man had been sitting. "So they agreed, no appeal."

In unison, Marcus and Bob said "Wow," staring at each other. Lisa was smiling broadly.

And then Bob started laughing. "When I grow up, I want to be a lawyer just like you."

They all had a merry lunch at The Harvest. After they ordered drinks and food, Bob went to a pay phone to call his dad and tell him what had happened.

Over dessert, Marcus looked worried, and Bob noticed. "What, what? You just won a major victory."

"Why hasn't Harvard announced the results of the plagiarism investigation?"

Lisa swallowed a mouthful of chocolate mousse she was guiltily eating and said that she would bet money they were waiting to see what happened today.

"Think of it this way. This will be hard for Harvard. They just tenured Deena. They have few enough tenured women as it is. If she's found guilty of plagiarism, it's a major black eye for them."

"I suppose," was all Marcus could think to say. "So much for veritas." *Veritas* was Harvard's simple motto: Truth.

Outside, Marcus thanked Lisa and hugged her. It was still freezing, so none of them lingered. Bob went to his office, and Marcus went home and collapsed on the bed.

"Thank God," he said before drifting off.

56

Marcus spent the rest of January—a reading and exam period at Harvard—working on his research, which was starting to come together, at least a little, and preparing his spring term courses. He also bought himself a cookbook and tried to make a few dinners, determined not to let Bob continue to do most of the work in the kitchen.

Just before the new semester began, Bob invited some friends from Brown over, Jeff Cohen and Barbara Solomon. "I'll do the cooking," he said, after Marcus had ruined yet another dinner. "But I love you for trying," Bob quickly added. He had lost three pounds eating, or not eating, Marcus's cooking, but didn't tell him.

Bob's friends came over on a Friday night. All three had been active together in Brown's LGBT organization; they told war stories and exchanged news about mutual friends. And they talked about a mini-course Bob had helped organize about the AIDS crisis, something Bob had never mentioned. Listening, Marcus once again recognized that Bob was a person of both substance and wit, and asked himself, not for the first time, how he had ever gotten so lucky.

Jeff was working at Boston's AIDS Action Committee; he handed them a flyer about a fundraiser that was coming up in a couple of weeks. They said they'd be there for sure.

Classes began the first full week of February, along with the usual rush to get syllabi ready, answer student questions, arrange reserve reading at the library. Marcus thought, not for the first time, that for a rich institution staff support for faculty seemed distressingly light.

During the second week of classes, while he was preparing a lecture, the phone rang in Marcus's office. It was Ralph Sedgwick from the *Crimson*, asking Marcus to comment on the plagiarism verdict against Professor Echols. Marcus said he had no comment.

How completely typical, Marcus thought. *No one even bothered to tell me what had transpired, but the* Crimson *already knows.*

He called the dean's office and asked the most human of the assistants about the plagiarism investigation. She put him on hold for what seemed like forever and then the dean came on the line.

"Professor George. The finding of the committee is that Professor Echols was guilty of not properly acknowledging her sources, and that this was a case of unintentional plagiarism due to technical difficulties. Professor Echols has been placed on administrative leave for one semester. She has agreed to issue a public apology and to ask her publisher to issue a corrected edition of the book in question. She has also agreed not to pursue any further action against you, and will excuse herself from any future personnel evaluation concerning your status here, or anywhere else."

"Thanks ever so much for letting me know," Marcus replied, and hung up.

Unintentional, my ass, he thought. But at least she wasn't let off scot-free. He wondered if the administrative leave was with or without pay. If it was with pay it was no punishment at all, but was in effect an extra semester of sabbatical.

Marcus called Lisa Rosenthal, told her the news, and asked her if he should make any kind of public statement. No, nothing, she advised. "Take this as a victory." He wasn't happy with that, but knew it was the right thing to do. He then called the *Crimson* and asked Sedgwick, off the record, about the leave. It was without pay.

"Well, that's something," he murmured to himself after getting off the phone.

He called Bob and told him they were going out to dinner to celebrate. They drove into Boston and went to Rebecca's, an upscale bistro at the foot of Beacon Hill. Being on the Hill made their thoughts turn to the Howards.

"Will they ever find out what happened to their son?" Bob asked.

"It doesn't look like it."

The article in the *Crimson* the next day about the plagiarism verdict was circumspect but gave all the major facts. It also contained a statement from the Harvard Women's Caucus, a faculty organization Marcus did not know existed. They said they believed Professor Echols had done nothing wrong and should have been fully exonerated. Undergraduate women were circulating a petition to that effect, which, Marcus knew, would have no impact. Undergraduates were paid even less attention than junior faculty.

Marcus ran into Rachel Hoffman in the hallway that afternoon. "Glad it's over. Nose to the grindstone," she said, which was abrupt, even for her.

When he got back to his office Marcus laughed and shook his head.

57

Marcus resumed eating in public, including at the Faculty Club on occasion. The glares seemed to have subsided, although there were still a few here and there. His colleague Julie Gordon invited him to lunch and apologized for being rude to him months prior when they had run into each other at Steve's.

"I rushed to judgment. I shouldn't have done that. I'm so sorry."

Marcus thanked her, and they turned to the usual Harvard gossip.

He threw himself into his teaching and, when he could snatch the time, his writing. He was feeling content, or as content as he could as an untenured faculty member at an institution without a tenure-track system.

He was teaching a tutorial, "American Fiction as Political Thought," and the second half of "American Political Rhetoric," which started with World War II and went to the present. It was the course he loved best, covering the 1950s, the anti-Communist hysteria, the Beat poets, the convulsions of the 1960s, feminism, gay liberation, civil rights, and everything that came after. It was a popular course with students clamoring to get in. He kept the enrollment at fifty so that it was possible to have at least a modicum of discussion. As usual during the semester, he didn't have much time or energy for his own work, but at this particular moment, he didn't much mind.

At the end of February, in the middle of a typical Boston blizzard, Marcus trudged home through deep snow and wind, wanting nothing more than to snuggle with Bob on the couch. Then he remembered that night was the AIDS fundraiser they had agreed to attend. They had paid $100 each for the tickets.

"Shit," he said out loud.

Bob came home and they made a quick light meal of leftovers. They showered and changed, put on their warmest coats, and dug out one of their cars. The snow was still coming down hard.

The fundraiser was at a townhouse in the South End, which had become Boston's gayborhood; Beacon Hill, the Back Bay, and even Cambridge had grown too expensive. They were relieved to see there was valet parking and surrendered the car. They mounted the steps to the house and before they could knock, a handsome young man in a bow tie opened the door.

"Straight from central casting," Bob whispered.

There were similar young men circulating with finger food. The place was large, packed, and noisy.

Jeff Cohen, Bob's college chum, found them, hugged them both, and told them to have fun. "I'm trying to put the moves on a Yalie," he said. "Wish me luck." He crossed the room, looking determined.

The townhouse had been renovated beautifully and there was still the faint smell of fresh paint. It was expensively furnished, with glass and art everywhere. They made their way to the bar and asked for red wine. After a while Jeff came and found them again.

"No luck?" Bob asked.

"No." Jeff frowned. "What can you expect from Yale? I was doing fine until I told him I went to Brown. I mean, really."

Bob asked which of the many gay men there was their host. Jeff pointed to the far side of the room.

"Back there. That number with all the muscle, surrounded by twinks."

It was hard to see, what with all the circulating bodies, but Marcus caught a brief glimpse of an attractive man in an expensive suit. He wore no tie, and his shirt was opened to reveal a muscular chest, the kind that required daily visits to the gym. He did indeed have several beautiful young men hanging on his every word. He put his arm around one of them, and Marcus could see what looked like a Rolex on his wrist and an expensive ring.

"What's his name? What does he do?" Bob asked.

"Joel something. Doesn't do anything. Apparently loaded. Just moved to Boston." Jeff pointed to another young man. "Okay, that one went to Michigan. Maybe I have a chance." He set off in hot pursuit.

Bob and Marcus both laughed as they watched him, each silently thanking the Almighty that they had found each other.

A tipsy man in a business suit and a loosened tie covered with the Harvard crest approached Marcus and hugged him.

"Marky, how have you been?"

"Oh fine, fine." Marcus was embarrassed but tried not to show it. "This is my partner, Bob."

The stranger gave Bob the once over. "Hmm, nice. Hold on to this one," the drunk said to Marcus. He moved on, and

Bob smirked.

"So, Marky. Hmm?"

"What can I say. A youthful indiscretion."

"You mean you weren't a virgin when we met? I am shocked, shocked."

When they finished their wine, Bob said, "Well, we've been here thirty minutes, at least. Mom and Miss Manners say that's the minimum amount of time to stay at any event. Let's go home before more of your sordid past comes calling."

Marcus was more than happy to oblige.

As they handed their parking ticket to the young man at the door, Marcus turned and tried to get another look at the host but couldn't see him.

Their car came and they made it back to Cambridge alive, despite the slippery roads and the snow. The streets were all but deserted. In the apartment, Bob pulled out some of Ruth's brownies that had arrived that week and made a pot of decaf. The brownies were slightly stale but still delicious.

Bob was in an amorous mood when they turned in. As they were cuddling and drifting off to sleep, Marcus said "Let's drive up to the beach tomorrow."

"You're demented. It's too cold."

"Come on, it'll be fun." From some place in the back of his mind, he didn't know why, Marcus felt an urge to go back to Miller's Cove.

58

In the morning Marcus called and found an inn that was still open and even had a room with a fireplace. When he heard that, Bob relented.

They drove up late Saturday morning, had lunch at Maineium's, then went back to their room and built a fire. They both read and felt wonderfully peaceful. It was snowing softly. The innkeepers, a friendly straight couple, said they would cook dinner for them and serve it in the dining room, which also had a fireplace. They made a feast, lobster bisque and tender chicken in a heavenly sauce, and pumpkin pie for dessert with good strong coffee. There didn't seem to be any other guests.

On Sunday they took a walk around town despite the cold. Many of the shops were closed, and they stopped in front of The Club and noticed that it had a fancy new sign.

"Next summer," Bob said, "you're going to take me dancing there at least three times."

Marcus laughed. "Yes, sir."

They drove back to Cambridge in the afternoon, wanting to get home before dark. They ordered pizza then went to bed early and cuddled.

Just as Bob was falling asleep, Marcus sat bolt upright.

"What's the matter?" Bob asked, alarmed.

Marcus knew where he had seen the host of the fundraiser in the South End. He was Joe, the bartender at The Club.

59

They jumped out of bed and pulled on clothes and went into the kitchen. Bob made tea. Marcus paced.

"What is someone who worked as a bartender in Miller's Cove doing with a new townhouse in Boston? And hosting a fundraiser, wearing expensive clothes and jewelry?"

"He came into some money," Bob said, trying to sound hopeful.

"And how does someone come into money like that?" Marcus asked, pacing furiously.

"A rich relative dies. Happens all the time."

"Or," Marcus said, standing suddenly still, "he was paid for a service."

"Marcus . . ."

"A service like killing someone."

They stared at each other. Marcus stopped pacing and sat down. Bob poured the tea.

"Marcus . . ."

"The police should check it out, don't you think? They can find out where the money came from. Maybe it's legit. Maybe it isn't."

Bob nodded slightly in a way that Marcus had come to know meant okay. Bob was relieved that Marcus mentioned the police and wasn't planning on investigating himself. They each took a gulp of tea, and then Bob set his mug down hard.

"Marcus, did he see you? When we were there? At the townhouse."

Marcus looked at him.

"No. I don't think so. Why would that matter?"

"Because you've been snooping all over asking questions. And you had talked to him about Trip at The Club, right?"

Marcus gripped his own mug. "Yes. But we were way across the room at the townhouse. I could barely see his face, and he was busy putting the moves on that boy. Besides, to him I was just one more guy at The Club last summer." Marcus wasn't at all sure of that, but didn't want to alarm Bob.

"Marcus—"

"It was a crowded party. We were far away. He was busy. I'm not young and hot, so I'm not the kind of person he'd remember."

"Not so young, maybe, but as for hot ..." Bob gazed ruefully at him and walked into the bedroom. Marcus followed.

They went back to bed and clung to each other. Trip's murder had mercifully receded for both of them, and here it was, roaring back. They had a restless night, both wondering if this would ever end.

In the morning Marcus called the Miller's Cove police station and said he needed to speak to Lieutenant Fitzgerald immediately about a murder investigation. Fitzgerald called back from home a few minutes later, and Marcus told him what had happened. He tried to stick to facts, not to speculate, but Fitzgerald was way ahead of him.

"So maybe he was blackmailing Trip Howard over drugs, or sex, or something" Fitzgerald said. "Or maybe he was paid to murder him."

Marcus was glad, in a macabre sort of way, that Fitzgerald was seeing what he was seeing, at least as a possibility.

Fitzgerald continued. "They knew each other, so it wouldn't have been hard for this guy to get Trip to go for a walk on the Fourth of July."

Joe the bartender was Joseph Potenza, not Joel, Fitzgerald said. He was originally from Buffalo. The Miller's Cove police had interviewed him during the early stages of the investigation, and discovered possible mob connections in his background.

Fitzgerald thanked Marcus for his report. "This is important. It could be the break we're looking for. I'll turn your information over to the FBI."

"Please keep me posted. I don't know if he saw me at that party, but he may remember me, and he lives all of two miles away. If he's dangerous—"

"I'll let you know as soon as I have more information, Professor. Since Potenza is now in Boston, this is definitely FBI. Meanwhile, be very careful."

Marcus went into the bedroom and found Bob packing a suitcase.

"Where are you going?"

"We. We're going to Danbury until we know more."

"We can't leave. I have classes. You have work. This may all be nothing."

Bob plopped on the bed, put his head in his hands, and started to cry. Marcus sat next to him and took him in his arms.

"Don't cry. Please don't cry. Bobby, I love you. We'll be fine."

Bob blew his nose. "I love you too. But we're going to Danbury."

Marcus didn't try to argue.

60

There was something else that worried Marcus, although he kept it to himself. Did Potenza work alone? If he was a murderer, could he have had an accomplice, and could that accomplice try to hurt them or threaten them in some way?

One morning when leaving the apartment a few weeks before, Marcus thought he'd seen someone loitering in front of the building. The guy was young and muscular, like Joe Potenza, someone perhaps more at home in the Italian North End of Boston than in genteel Cambridge. Marcus thought the loiterer might have stared at him as he exited the building.

A needle of fear descended from his neck to his spine. At the time Marcus had told himself he was being paranoid, that the loiterer could be a grad student wondering about a newly vacant apartment, or a repairman, or anyone, really; the street had lots of foot traffic. Still, as they drove south to Danbury, he wondered.

They got there in time for lunch. Ruth fed them chicken sandwiches while she and Jake listened to their story.

Jake scratched his head. "So you think . . ."

"I don't know," Marcus said. "All I know is a bartender who knew Trip appears to suddenly have a lot of money."

Ruth was thinking. "And if he saw you at the party . . ."

Clearly, Bob shared more of his mother than just some of her looks. "Exactly," Bob said.

"Bob is right," Jake said. "This is dangerous. Stay here until you know more."

"But my classes—"

"Call in sick. Both of you. It's February. Say you have the flu. What could be more believable?"

Bob nodded. The look on his face, Marcus knew, meant he had made up his mind.

"Okay," Marcus said. "Until we know more, at least."

Once that was settled, they all relaxed. Marcus called Fitzgerald's office and left a message with the Danbury phone number.

"Now," Ruth said, back to her usual cheerful self, "who wants to play Scrabble?"

61

They both called in sick on Monday morning. Marcus went to the Danbury library with Ruth's card and was able to find a few of the books he needed to get some work done, although he found himself reading some of the same paragraphs over and over. At home Bob and Ruth cooked and baked all day.

When Marcus got back from the library in the late afternoon, an agitated Bob greeted him at the door and said Fitzgerald had just called.

Marcus called back right away.

The FBI had picked Potenza up for questioning and had issued a subpoena for his financial records. Fitzgerald said he expected to have more news the next day.

Jake came home early and they sat down for dinner. Marcus was so preoccupied he didn't even notice what they were eating or watching on television after dinner. They all went to bed early.

On Tuesday, Jake went to work and Ruth, Bob, and Marcus stuck around the house, waiting for the phone to ring and trying not to make each other nervous. Marcus sat with a book but couldn't concentrate. Bob made brownies and burned them. Ruth was up in the attic cleaning, a sure sign, Bob said, that she was worried.

Finally the phone rang. It was Fitzgerald. Potenza's money came from an offshore bank account that looked suspicious, he said. The FBI was going after that company's records and was at that moment searching Potenza's Boston townhouse. Fitzgerald said he'd call that evening with an update.

At dinner it was as if they were waiting for a baby to be born; everyone was in that altered state composed of equal parts anxiety and anticipation. Nothing much else existed but what was about to happen.

After dinner, Marcus paced. Bob kept pulling him down to the couch, but he would pop back up and pace some more.

"He does this all the time," Bob said to Ruth.

At nine o'clock that night, Fitzgerald called again. Ruth handed the phone to Marcus, and they all gathered round.

The FBI had found a gun at the townhouse that matched the make and model of the gun used on July Fourth. A ballistics test revealed that there was a ninety-six percent certainty that it was the gun that killed Trip Howard.

They arrested Potenza for first-degree murder.

"My God," Marcus said when he got off the phone. He told them what he had just heard, and everyone let out a breath.

"Thank the Lord," Ruth said. "It's over."

62

Marcus and Bob drove back to Cambridge early on Wednesday and went back to work, greatly relieved, but both realized there was still a huge piece missing from the story: Potenza's motive. Had he been blackmailing Trip? Or was he paid by someone else, someone who wanted Trip dead? They tried not to obsess about the case, but it was like trying not to think about an approaching hurricane. Impossible.

The Boston winter was fierce that year, and just getting from place to place and staying warm took up most of their energy. At dinner they'd tell each other about their work and then they'd snuggle on the couch. Bob forced Marcus to watch popular movies, telling him again that his cinema education had been sorely neglected. When Marcus said he had never seen a Lana Turner movie, Bob said, "That's it. I'm calling gay central. You're on probation. There will be quizzes."

A week passed before Fitzgerald called again, reaching Marcus at his office.

"There's more news, and it will be a shock. All around."

Marcus felt very calm, that scary, something-awful-is-happening kind of calm.

"The money in that offshore account came from an investment holding company. The two officers of that company are David Howard and Jordan Echols."

It took a long moment for that to sink in.

"Are you saying David Howard and Jordan Echols paid that guy to murder Trip?" Marcus asked finally. He could hardly get the words out.

Marcus thought there must be some mistake, and his mind was racing. "How is that possible? Echols did this for Deena? To hide the plagiarism? And David did it for . . . what?"

Fitzgerald sighed. He explained that David and Jordan Echols knew each other well. They were in the same law school class and worked on some cases together when David was an attorney, before he was elected to the state house. They saw each other socially.

"But how did that lead to murder?" Marcus now felt dizzy.

"Trip Howard apparently confronted Deena Echols about the plagiarism right after the Harvard graduation, in June. As you suggested. Deena obviously told Jordan about it."

"And Jordan went to David," Marcus said.

"Yes. Of course, Jordan knew Trip was David's brother. Jordan and David were in business together—that offshore investment company. The two couples were close. Deena was becoming thick with Caroline, David's fiancée."

Caroline Peters, that was her name. Marcus remembered the large engagement ring she was wearing at Trip's memorial service, and that she and David had just spent a few days in France. He could imagine Deena wanting to be a good friend to a very rich woman.

And Marcus suddenly remembered something else. It had been Jordan having lunch with David that day at the

Harvard club in Boston, when Marcus met the elder Mr. Howard.

Fitzgerald went on. "David Howard was already planning to blackmail his brother. He had located Potenza and hired him to do the dirty work."

"How?" Marcus asked. He was still not believing what he was hearing.

"David hired a low-rent private detective to find a shady character in the gay community, someone who could threaten Trip, and the sleazy detective found out Potenza was dealing drugs in the club, along with some guy from Portland."

Marcus remembered "Smith" in the parking lot.

"The Boston police know about that detective. He's a real low-life. But he hasn't broken any laws. That's how David got Potenza to blackmail Trip for a relatively small amount of money; he threatened to turn Potenza over to the police for drug dealing. A real charmer, that David."

"But why did David think Trip could be blackmailed? And why would he need more money than he already had?" It still made no sense to Marcus.

"I'm getting there. David knew Trip would be upset if his parents found out about his sleeping around, his drug use. The parents, especially Howard Senior, still hadn't completely accepted the fact that Trip was ... you know, gay."

Marcus could believe that.

"And apparently there was some clause in the trust fund that could have allowed the Howards to cut off Trip's money, at least until his twenty-fifth birthday, for illegal or immoral behavior."

"I see." Marcus closed his eyes. "So that was the leverage. A morals clause in a trust fund."

"Yes. And then Echols chimed in, and David saw an

opportunity to make even more money. He was willing to include a threat about Deena in the scheme. In return, Jordan gave up a percentage of his equity in the investment firm. Not a huge percentage, but David, apparently, was desperate, any amount helped."

"But what was David's motive?" It still made no sense to Marcus. "Just greed? He was already so rich." Marcus's head was still spinning.

"Even the rich can have money problems, Professor," Fitzgerald responded. "The offshore company made some very bad choices over the last few years and lost a fortune as a result. At one point, they lost nearly $10 million, much of it David's own money."

Marcus gulped. "That's a lot."

"Yes. David was strapped, and, apparently, desperate, especially since he was about to marry a woman used to a certain lifestyle."

"But his own income—"

"Caroline Peters is from one of the richest families in California. Hollywood money on one side, oil money on the other. There are rich families, like the Howards, and then there's the super-rich. Her family is super-rich."

"And?"

"And David was trying to keep up. The two of them were constantly flying off to Europe or wherever, hanging out with the jet set. They were planning to buy various homes. All that takes a lot of cash. And then the investment losses . . ."

Fitzgerald didn't finish the sentence.

Marcus felt like he was watching a car accident in slow motion.

"And you said yourself," Fitzgerald went on, "the

plagiarism could have ruined Deena."

"Oh, God," Marcus said. It was all he could think of.

"Once David knew we were onto him and had arrested Potenza," Fitzgerald continued, "he confessed to everything, explained it all. The plan was just to have Potenza rough up the younger brother a little bit and blackmail him, based on his drug use and his lifestyle. Potenza would have kept David's name out of it and would have been paid his fee. David would have gotten most of Trip's money. And Potenza would have warned Trip to forget about the plagiarism for good measure. Potenza would have gone on dealing drugs."

Fitzgerald put the phone down for a moment to speak to someone, then came back. "Anyway, that was the plan. Blackmail, not murder. But . . ."

"But?"

"But on July Fourth, Trip apparently told Potenza to get lost, fought back. We think things got out of hand, and Potenza just lost it and used his gun."

Marcus closed his eyes. "So an accident?"

"That will be for a prosecutor and a jury to decide. After the shooting, Potenza demanded a lot more than his fee, a fortune, in fact, enough to set himself up for a long time. Both David and Jordan Echols paid. So—"

"So the townhouse in the South End," Marcus interrupted. Then, after a brief silence, he asked whether the parents had been informed.

"The FBI is doing that right now."

Marcus tried to imagine the scene, then thought of something else. He asked whether Deena was part of the conspiracy.

"She claims she had no knowledge of the offshore money, or the blackmail scheme, or anything else. Jordan is saying the same thing. Jordan is in custody. The FBI is questioning both of them at length. Jordan is a lawyer, and he probably knew how to give Deena deniability. It's quite possible he didn't tell her."

Marcus thanked Fitzgerald for everything, hung up, and put his head on his desk. He felt dizzy, disoriented.

But he had gotten what he wanted. The puzzle had been solved.

He knew.

63

Over the next few weeks, lurid stories appeared in the press, featuring every detail about the Howard family that reporters could find, together with details about Jordan and Deena and the plagiarism case. In Boston the story was headline news for days on end. There were pictures of Mr. and Mrs. Howard in dark sunglasses as they walked to a limousine in front of the Beacon Hill townhouse, press hounding them at every side. There were pictures of the Kennebunkport house and details about the family's wealth and lineage. The Vice President was asked for a comment and declined to say anything.

Deena was already on administrative leave from Harvard. She filed for divorce from Jordan, announced a second edition of her book acknowledging Dorothy Edgerly's writing, and stepped down from all her other professional involvements. Pictures of her, also in dark sunglasses, showed her leaving her Cambridge house with a suitcase. The press said she was in seclusion in Washington with her parents.

Marcus taught his classes, ate lunch at his desk, and mostly worked at home. He offered a terse "no comment" to the *Crimson*, *The Boston Globe*, and *The New York Times*, as did university officials.

Not a soul on campus talked to Marcus directly about the case or reacted in any way that he could see, except Rachel Hoffman, who knocked on his office door one day, came in, patted him on the back, and left without a word.

Potenza, it turned out, had a record of low-level extortion as well as drug dealing. He quickly cut a deal and pleaded guilty to second-degree murder with a sentence of twenty years. Jordan Echols was charged with conspiracy to commit murder and also took a deal, pleading guilty to extortion. He received a sentence of ten years. David Howard decided to take his chances with a jury and was awaiting trial.

64

The phone rang one evening at Kirkland Street, and Mr. Howard invited Marcus to tea. He'd been afraid an invitation from the Howards was coming, and he didn't want to go but couldn't think of a way to refuse. So on a wet Thursday in late March, he once again took the T to Louisburg Square.

The butler admitted him, and Mr. Howard greeted him in the entrance hall and took him into the parlor. Mrs. Howard was sitting in front of the fire and did not get up; she smiled faintly. She wore black slacks and a black sweater with no jewelry.

The butler brought a tea tray.

"Would you like something stronger?" Mr. Howard asked. "Scotch, or sherry?"

"Actually yes, sherry would be very nice, thanks."

There was an awkward silence. Finally Marcus spoke.

"I'm so sorry things worked out the way they did. I can't imagine how difficult all this must be for you."

Now it was Mr. Howard who had the faraway look in his eyes. "We just wish David had come to us for financial help."

Mrs. Howard did not speak or look at her husband. Her expression was blank. She had aged five years in just a few short months, Marcus thought, or perhaps she was wearing less makeup.

"We want you to know," Mr. Howard said, choking back tears, "that we are grateful to you for helping us find out what happened to Trip."

Marcus nodded and finished his sherry. There was little more to say, so after a few minutes of small talk, it was time to go. The square outside was quiet, the reporters gone, apparently thanks to the intervention of Senator Kerry, who lived across the way.

On the way home on the T, Marcus put his head in his hands. He couldn't remember ever feeling so tired. He was tired of the rich and he was tired of Ivy League games, all of it. He was bone tired.

Then he lifted his head and thought about Bob and Ruth and Jake.

Bob knew Marcus would be upset that evening and did everything he could to take care of him, including making his favorite dinner, lasagna. He didn't even make him watch a movie.

Marcus fell asleep in his arms. "We need to leave here, when you finish school. Go someplace else, start fresh," he said, as he drifted off.

Bob smiled and rubbed his back. "Okay."

65

David Howard went on trial, was found guilty of being an accessory to second-degree murder and attempted extortion, and was sentenced to fifteen years in prison. Neither of his parents attended the trial, which was extensively covered in the local and national press. In the photos of David walking into the courthouse, he too looked like he had aged since the last time Marcus saw him. The press hounded Caroline Peters, who said only that she had broken off her engagement. She took refuge in the South of France and had no further comment.

"Thank God it's over. Really over," Marcus said to Bob when they heard the news about the verdict against David.

They got on with their lives. They tried to forget, but both knew that was impossible.

They seldom spoke of what had happened. Marcus got his three years as an associate professor and worked on his book. They rented a house in Miller's Cove in the summer, and Marcus spent most of his time under the awning, in the shade.

66

After David's trial, Mr. and Mrs. Howard divorced. About a year after the divorce was final, Mrs. Howard, living alone in the Louisburg Square townhouse, gave the servants the night off and shot herself through the mouth with a handgun. The butler found her the next morning.

Mr. Howard quickly remarried a much younger woman and they spent most of their time in Kennebunkport.

Deena Echols was never charged with a crime; the FBI concluded that they did not have evidence to charge her with anything. She eventually returned to teaching, accepting a chair at Macalester College in Minnesota.

A few weeks after Mrs. Howard's death, Marcus received a certified letter from her attorney. In her will, she had left him the Kandinsky that had hung over the mantle in the parlor on Beacon Hill. Tucked into the frame when the painting arrived was an unsigned note on the family's heavy, cream-colored stationery. It contained one line.

"I forgive you."

Acknowledgments

Heartfelt thanks to editors Priscilla Long and Joy Johannessen, to Ana Cara, Sandra Zagarell, and Tom van Nortwick for reading drafts, to Sarah Schulman for sage advice, and to A.D. Reed of Pisgah Press for thinking this work should see the light of day.

This is a work of fiction. Aside from the brief mentions of public figures, no true events or real individuals are depicted.

TURN THE PAGE FOR ...

a preview of H. N. Hirsch's next exciting mystery featuring Marcus and Bob, *Fault Line*, coming in 2023 from Pisgah Press.

Coming in 2023 from Pisgah Press

Fault Line

by H. N. Hirsch

On his first day in California, Bob Abramson awoke to an earthquake, rain, and murder.

The clock radio went off just as a mellow California voice was announcing "a small earthquake." Marcus must have set the alarm, Bob realized, although why, he couldn't fathom. Bob had flown in the night before, a Friday. Marcus had scurried to come out a few days sooner to meet the movers, who arrived ahead of schedule from the East.

When Bob heard "earthquake," he bolted out of bed. Having grown up and gone to school on the East coast, he was terrified of earthquakes, not to mention mud slides and fires, all the things he knew were possible beneath the placid, gorgeous surface of Southern California.

He glanced around the room, where nothing seemed to have moved, then peered out the window. A drizzle was coming down, but everything was still in place, all the houses and lawns and cars neat and tidy, just as they had been when they looked at the house a few months before.

His panic subsided.

He looked at the clock radio: 6:30. The mellow voice was explaining that the quake was "only" a 3.2, nothing to worry about, no damage reported. He trudged to the bathroom, tripping over an open suitcase.

When he came out he could smell Marcus's scrambled

eggs. He pulled on gym shorts and a T-shirt as he walked into the kitchen. He kissed the back of Marcus's neck and announced, "We've had a small earthquake."

"You mean last night?" Marcus smirked. Having been separated for a few days and exhausted with packing for a week before that, they both had been more than ready for sex.

Bob smiled. "No, a real one. It was on the radio. Three-point-two. I guess that counts as little. No damage. But what's with this rain? I thought this was sunny California."

Marcus chuckled as Bob added pepper to the eggs. Marcus always forgot the pepper.

"It's called June Gloom," Marcus said. "Someone explained it to me. The desert east of here heats up fast as summer comes on, pulls in mist from the ocean, so for a while there can be gray skies or drizzle. Or something like that. Topography. It can start in May and doesn't end until around now."

"My first day, rain and an earthquake."

"Don't be a grouch. There's coffee. This will be done in two minutes."

Marcus had met the movers, bought food, and made a start on painting. He decided on crisp yellow for their living room and a subtle blue in the kitchen; both rooms were half painted. The blue in the kitchen matched the set of lovely, expensive dishes Bob's parents had sent them, which were spread out all over the counters. Bob stared at them and felt a pang; he had never lived this far from his parents and his childhood home.

He poured himself a cup of coffee and stood at the open door to the patio. He peered out at the yard of their new house and inhaled: orange blossoms, sweet and a bit soapy. Freshly cut grass. The drizzle felt peaceful.

He smiled again. He could get used to this, he thought to himself. The air was never sweet in Boston. If you were lucky, it didn't carry the smell of car exhaust.

He heard a thump at the front door and realized Marcus must have started delivery of the local newspaper. He retrieved it and pulled it out of the blue plastic wrapper as he walked back into the kitchen. He opened the paper and was stunned by a huge headline in bold type:

MAYOR'S HUSBAND FOUND DEAD

Mystery Fans:
If you would like to be notified when Fault Line *will be available for purchase, please send your email address to PisgahPress@gmail.com with "Fault Line" as the subject.*

About the Author

H. N. Hirsch was born in Chicago and educated at the University of Michigan and at Princeton. A political scientist by training, he has been on the faculties of Harvard, the University of California-San Diego, Macalester College, and Oberlin, where he served as Dean of the Faculty and is now the Erwin N. Griswold Professor of Politics Emeritus. He is the author of *The Enigma of Felix Frankfurter* ("brilliant and sure to be controversial" —*The New York Times*), *A Theory of Liberty*, and the memoir *Office Hours* ("well crafted and wistful" —Kirkus), and numerous articles on law, politics, and constitutional questions.

About Pisgah Press

Pisgah Press was established in 2011 in Asheville, NC to publish works of quality offering original ideas and insight into the human condition and the world around us. Ifl you support the old-fashioned tradition of publishing for the pleasure of the reader and the benefit of the author, please encourage your friends and colleagues to visit www.PisgahPress.com. For more information about *Shade* and other Pisgah Press books, contact us at pisgahpress@gmail.com.

Also available from Pisgah Press

Gabriel's Songbook Michael Amos Cody
$17.95 **FINALIST, FEATHERED QUILL BOOK AWARD, FICTION, 2021**
A Twilight Reel
$17.95 **GOLD MEDALIST, FEATHERED QUILL BOOK AWARD, SHORT STORIES, 2021**

Letters of the Lost Children: Japan—WWII Reinhold C. Ferster
$37.95 & Jan Atchley Bevan

Musical Morphine: Transforming Pain One Note at a Time Robin Russell Gaiser
$17.95 **FINALIST, USA BOOK AWARDS, 2017**
Open for Lunch
$17.95

LANKY TALES C. Robert Jones
Lanky Tales, Vol. I: The Bird Man & other stories
$9.00
Lanky Tales, Vol. II: Billy Red Wing & other stories
$9.00
Lanky Tales, Vol. III: A Good and Faithful Friend & other stories
$9.00
The Mystery at Claggett Cove
$9.00

The Last of the Swindlers Peter Loewer
$17.95

Homo Sapiens: A Violent Gene? Mort Malkin
$22.95

Reed's Homophones: A Comprehensive Book of Sound-alike Words A.D. Reed
$17.95

Swords in their Hands: George Washington and the Newburgh Conspiracy Dave Richards
$24.95 **FINALIST, USA BOOK AWARDS, HISTORY, 2014**

Trang Sen: A Novel of Vietnam Sarah-Ann Smith
$19.50

Invasive Procedures: Earthquakes, Calamities, & poems from the midst of life Nan Socolow
$17.95

Deadly Dancing THE RICK RYDER MYSTERY SERIES RF Wilson
$15.95
Killer Weed
$14.95
The Pot Professor
$17.95

To order:

Pisgah Press, LLC
PO Box 9663, Asheville, NC 28815
www.pisgahpress.com

CPSIA information can be obtained
at www.ICGtesting.com
Printed in the USA
BVHW030151090622
639335BV00011B/212

unigénito, que nació de la virgen María, para morir por mí y llevar mi juicio en la cruz. Creo que resucitó al tercer día y ahora está sentado a tu diestra como mi Señor y Salvador. Por lo tanto, en este día me arrepiento de mi independencia de ti y entrego mi vida eternamente al señorío de Jesús.

Jesús, te confieso como mi Señor y Salvador. Entra en mi vida mediante tu Espíritu y transfórmame en un hijo de Dios. Renuncio a las cosas de las tinieblas a las que antes me aferraba, y desde este día en adelante ya no viviré para mí mismo. Por tu gracia, viviré para ti que te entregaste por mí para que pueda vivir para siempre.

Gracias, Señor; mi vida está ahora por completo en tus manos, y según tu Palabra, nunca seré avergonzado. En el nombre de Jesús, amén.

¡Bienvenido a la familia de Dios! Te aliento a que compartas tu buena noticia con otro creyente. También es importante que te unas a una iglesia local que crea en la Biblia y conectes con otros que puedan alentarte en tu nueva fe.

Acabas de embarcarte en el viaje más asombroso. ¡Que puedas crecer en revelación, gracia y amistad con Dios cada día!